Praise for Malcolm Rose's

KISS OF DEATH

**Selected for the national Booked Up scheme and
shortlisted for the Sheffield, Manchester,
Bolton and Lancashire Children's Book Awards
and the Salisbury Schools' Book Award**

"An enthralling read."   *Books for Keeps*

"This is a really gripping story – I couldn't put it
down. It is fast-paced, full of nail-biting moments
and more than one shock – not for the squeamish."
Primary Times

"A disturbingly thrilling story."   *Northern Echo*

"This is a disturbing, spine-chilling novel that will
put you on the edge of your seat, terrified to read the
next page... A truly thrilling read and a fantastic
novel."   Laura Burke, aged 13, *Cork Evening Echo*

"This is a subject that will appeal to anyone who
likes the gory bits of history and enjoys a good
ghost story."   www.book~~~~~~.uk

"Brings the past in   the
present."   an

FORBIDDEN ISLAND

MALCOLM ROSE

USBORNE

With thanks to
Karen, Denis and the Wellwisher
for their unending hospitality and enthusiasm

First published in the UK in 2009 by Usborne Publishing Ltd., Usborne House, 83-85 Saffron Hill, London EC1N 8RT, England. www.usborne.com

Copyright © Malcolm Rose, 2009

The right of Malcolm Rose to be identified as the author of this work has been asserted by him in accordance with the Copyright, Designs and Patents Act, 1988.

Cover photography: Helicopter © Jehad Nga/Corbis; clouds billowing over hill © David Gray/Reuters/Corbis.

The name Usborne and the devices ♀ ⊕ are Trade Marks of Usborne Publishing Ltd.

A CIP catalogue record for this book is available from the British Library.

JFMAMJ ASOND/09   92478   9780746098639

Printed in the UK by J F Print Ltd., Sparkford, Somerset.

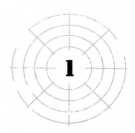

1

"There's land ahead!" Mike shouted above the growl of the motor.

"Don't be stupid," said Hugh as he steered the boat south. The Scottish island of Mull had disappeared behind them some time ago and they were still a long way from the islands in front. "There's no land out here. Not according to the map." Keeping his hands on the wheel, he nodded towards the GPS screen attached to the sunshade, next to the boat's radio.

Unsteady on his feet, Mike gripped the fibreglass canopy with one hand and pointed with the other. "What's that then?"

They all screwed up their eyes to peer across the sea. There was certainly something ahead, where there should have been only water and waves.

"Maybe it's a trick of the light," said Hugh's girlfriend, Lauren. "People crossing a desert sometimes see water that's not there. Maybe we're seeing land that's not there."

"Like we're all going to see the same mirage," Annie replied. "Looks pretty solid to me."

"Now you mention it… But…" Hugh tapped the chart above his head.

"Not on the map, eh?" Mike replied. "Fantastic. We can be the first ever human beings to explore a secret island. Set a new course, captain!"

Hugh groaned.

Annie thumped her brother playfully on the shoulder. "Come on, Hugh. Mike's right. It'll be fun."

"Okay."

It was crazy but, as they got closer, no one could deny that they were approaching an island. It wasn't enormous and it certainly wasn't mountainous, but it was there. At a distance, there were no signs of life. No trees, no houses, no movement. There didn't seem to be any beaches either. It was just a low dome of rock with patchy yellowed grass.

Over and over again, Hugh glanced at the electronic chart as if land might magically appear on it. But it didn't. He pressed a few buttons on the control panel and then shook his head in disbelief. "That's the satellite image of where we are. Nothing. I mean, how can a whole island – it must be a couple of kilometres across – not show up? That's not right."

The boat rose and fell as its prow cut through each wave. Holding onto Mike's arm, Annie said, "I heard a rumour that there was a haunted island out here somewhere. A ship got wrecked on it and all the crew were drowned. Everyone keeps away, so they say."

"Who's *they*?" said Hugh.

"You know. The locals," Annie explained.

"Huh," Hugh muttered. "Probably the same ones who talk about the Loch Ness monster."

Mike butted in. "It just keeps getting better. Hidden *and* haunted!"

"How do you explain the chart?" said Hugh. "It's just sea."

Mike shrugged. "Someone's fiddling with the satellite signal."

"Why?"

"I don't know."

"I do," Annie said with a big grin. "To keep the island secret."

Hugh sniggered at the idea, but it was clear from his face that he couldn't think of a better one.

On holiday in Scotland, Mike had run into Annie

and her family five days ago. Even though he was camping in a cheap tent and they were cruising in two boats between posh hotels on the west coast, he'd hit it off with Annie straight away. When Annie, her little brother Daniel, big brother Hugh and his girlfriend Lauren took their motor cruiser out for the day, Annie asked Mike to come too. Mike knew there was another sister as well, but apparently she wasn't invited – or maybe she just wasn't interested.

Annie told him that the small motor boat had been a joint birthday present for the four of them from their parents a couple of years earlier. Sometimes, it got left behind and they all went on the big motorized yacht. This time, they'd brought both boats to give them flexibility. Lingering in Oban for a week, Mr. and Mrs. Firth could use the yacht to go in one direction while the youngsters went somewhere else in the motor launch.

To Mike, Annie's parents seemed very trusting. They expected their kids to stay safe and be responsible. They didn't check out exactly where they were going or what they were doing. But there was a reason for the trust. Annie had told him that her family took to the sea every school holiday and quite a few weekends if the conditions were good, so the kids were very experienced. Also, the weather forecast for the day was ideal. Besides, they could always make contact over the boat's radio or use their mobile phones if there was an emergency. On top of that, Mike believed that Hugh had never done anything wrong or risky in his entire life. He was a sixteen-year-old who acted more like he was forty.

Standing apart from the rest of them, Annie's other brother, Daniel, gripped the rail at the stern and watched the approach to the mysterious, barren island. His face was crinkled with concern. At thirteen, he was younger than the rest. Maybe he also felt out of it because he didn't have a girlfriend.

A couple of hundred metres from the shore, Hugh let the engine idle while they took a good look. There were some rocky inlets and a few outcrops but nothing that welcomed a boat – not even a small one.

"Let's land," Mike said, the excitement clear in his voice.

"Be sensible," Hugh replied. "It's not like a bike you just jump off and prop against a wall, you know."

Annie was examining the shoreline through binoculars. "I can't see anything... Oh, hang on." She handed the binoculars to Hugh. "Along there. A few hundred metres. Isn't that some sort of jetty?"

"Mmm. If it is, it's knackered."

"It might not matter," Annie replied. "Let's go and find out."

The motor cruiser rocked gently as Hugh steered it parallel to the shore. Mike kept his eye on the land but he didn't spot any roads or even tracks. No animals stared back at him or ran away in fright. No birds were squatting in the nooks in the rock face. The place was strangely quiet and still.

Expertly, Hugh manoeuvred the boat alongside what remained of the small wooden jetty. "It's ruined," he said.

"But we can still use it," Annie replied.

"I don't like the look of it," Hugh said. "It's not just rotten. I think it's been wrecked – deliberately. Someone didn't want people landing..."

"The sea's bashed it about a bit, that's all," Mike said, not really knowing if it was true but eager to explore.

Lauren pointed to the left. "What's that, then?"

It was an old warning sign, lying on its side. It was dirty and worn, but part of it was still readable.

Danger. Keep away from this island.

2

Looking at the warning notice, Annie laughed. "Maybe we're not quite the first people to land here."

"It means there's something exciting somewhere," Mike said. "Let's go and find out what it is." Before Hugh could stop him, he jumped from the starboard side onto a sturdy beam that was still in place on the smashed jetty.

Mike didn't realize that the wooden girder would be slippery. He landed on the slimy surface, but the worn tread of his trainers didn't give him a firm foothold. His right foot slid off and he began to topple over.

He was about to plunge down between the slats and into the Atlantic Ocean when instinct came to his rescue. He grabbed an old rail. Luckily, the metal was rusty enough to provide a good grip, but not so corroded that it broke. He steadied himself and then turned to the others with a grin. "No problem. Come on, shipmates!"

Hugh sighed and said to his sister, "Where did you pick this joker up?"

Annie was quick to excuse her lively new boyfriend. "On dry land. He's a city boy, not used to boats."

"What do you mean?" Mike called back. "I watched *Pirates of the Caribbean* three times."

Mike liked Annie a lot but he didn't really feel part of her group. They were loaded and he was broke. Apart from Annie, they made him feel like a refugee. To make up for it, he joked around. He knew he was trying too hard but he couldn't help himself.

"Throw me the rope," he said. "I know you've got to tie boats up, even if the films were a bit hazy on how to do them smart sailor knots."

Annie grabbed the rope, which was coiled like a sleeping snake on the deck.

"Are you sure this is a good idea?" said Hugh.

"Come on. What harm can it do?" Mike replied.

Annie drew back her arm and flung the looped line towards him. Mike wound the end of it clumsily around the rail several times and then pulled it tight.

Within a few minutes, Lauren and Hugh had scrambled out onto the girder by heaving on the rope. After Hugh had moored the boat properly, they tottered along a warped metal support and joined Mike on the rock beside the shattered jetty. Daniel remained at the stern of the motor boat and didn't look keen to move at all. He gazed at the warning sign. "It says d-danger," he stammered.

Eager to join the others, Annie said to him, "It just means the landing's a bit rickety…"

"A bit rickety?"

"Dangerous, then. But we're hitched to it okay – thanks to Mike."

Daniel stayed stubbornly where he was.

Mike knew that Annie regarded herself as an expert at persuading Daniel. He stood at the edge of the rock and watched her at work.

"All right," she said to her brother. "It's up to you. Stay here while we go exploring." She made for the front, hesitated theatrically and then turned back towards him. "Remember *Jurassic Park*? The film with the flesh-eating dinosaurs. This island's just like it, isn't it? Without the steamy jungle. But you'll probably be okay on your own. If not, you can always scream for help. We *might* hear you."

"Mum and D-Dad wouldn't…"

Annie ignored Daniel's difficulty in saying words that began with d. She looked up and down the shoreline. "They don't seem to be here."

Muttering to himself, Daniel moved away from the rail. "I'll tell them when we get back. *If* we get back."

"Oh, don't spoil the fun, grumpy."

Standing on the island, Lauren looked at Daniel sympathetically for a moment before clasping Hugh's hand.

The island was as lifeless as it had appeared from the sea. But it wasn't as flat as they'd first thought. Away from the ocean, a rolling landscape with hidden dips lay in front of them. In places, the dark grey rock showed alarmingly deep cracks, sometimes wide enough to trap a careless foot. There were patches of grass, occasional clumps of hardy heather and gorse, and little else.

Lauren stopped and asked, "What are we looking for?"

Mike shrugged. "Anything. Fun."

"Okay. Let's head for the sports centre and cinema complex." Hugh glanced at his watch. "Maybe we should book a table at the restaurant."

"Restaurant?" Mike laughed. "What's wrong with a burger bar?"

It was midday and they'd left their packed lunches on the boat. Overhead, an angry sun scorched the island. Five half-hearted clouds barely stained the blue. The perfectly straight vapour trails from a high-flying military jet divided the sky like narrow ribbons. Slowly, the two white lines spread, touched and merged into one long fragile cloud. Then the dividing line evaporated altogether, banished by the sun's warmth.

"Let's carry on," Mike said, pointing further inland. "This way!" He set off again at speed, but tripped over almost at once. "Hey! What's that?"

His foot had caught on something metallic hidden in the grass. His fingers dug out a bulky chain, about two metres long with a brutal bracelet at the end. Getting up, he showed it to the others.

"Looks like a shackle to me," Hugh said. "A heavy-duty handcuff for trespassers like you."

Without opening the lock, Mike slipped the manacle over his hand and up his arm. "Too big for me." He yanked on the chain to show that it was firmly fixed into the rock below. "It'd hold a hippo back."

Still thinking about movies, Annie added with a wry grin, "Or a dinosaur."

Mike laughed again. "Maybe we've found a secret monster farm. They kept them locked up here till they were ready to let loose in Loch Ness." He let the chain go and it hit the ground with a loud clunk.

Daniel looked down at the metal restraint without a hint of a smile.

"I don't know," Lauren said, "but it's not nice, is it?" Her trousers and T-shirt were plain, smart and expensive. She was only out for a day trip in a boat but, as always, she looked elegant.

Hugh was carrying two bottles of water. He threw one to Annie. "For you and your stowaway." He held up the other and said, "For me and Lauren. Daniel gets a swig from both."

The island offered no shelter from the dazzling sunshine. The heat rippled the air and smudged the distance like a badly focused photograph.

Setting off for the centre of the island again, Daniel muttered to himself, "I wonder what this place is called."

Overhearing, Mike said, "Yeah, we should be allowed to give it a name. Mikeland or something."

"We're not the first to come here," Lauren reminded him. "Someone put that sign up, didn't they?"

Mike nodded. "And I suppose they made the hippo handcuff as well."

"If it's for a hippo," Annie said with a smile, "wouldn't it be a leg-cuff?"

"I still think we should be…" Daniel stopped. Once again, his head was down and he was staring at the ground.

"What now?"

They all gathered round. "Wow," Annie said. "Bones. Maybe a whole skeleton."

"Yeah. But what is it?" Mike asked. "Not a hippo or a dinosaur. Too small for that."

They all looked at Hugh. He shrugged. "I don't know. A cow or a pig?"

"I promised you something exciting," Mike said. "Pity it's not human. That'd be even better."

Annie picked up one of the bones. "At least it tells us the island used to have animals. One anyway."

"More than one," Lauren replied. With a look of horror on her face, she was gazing into a dip where another skeleton was attached to a post by a tether.

3

Hugh stood on a rock above the latest find. "It's smaller. A calf or a sheep or something."

"Maybe a biggish dog," Annie suggested.

"I wish I paid attention in science," said Mike.

Hugh bent down to touch the skeleton, but Lauren cried, "No!" Despite the heat, she shivered. "It's too creepy."

Hugh straightened up and took his girlfriend's hand. "Perhaps it's time we went back to—"

Mike butted in before Hugh could finish. "You've got to be joking! It's just getting interesting."

"But Lauren isn't—"

Mike interrupted again. "What do you think, Annie?"

"It's weird, for sure. But I want to know what happened here."

"That's right," Mike replied. "Come on. Let's look around. There's got to be an answer somewhere."

"It's so quiet," Daniel said.

They all stood still for a few seconds and listened. Daniel was right. They were now too far from the coast to hear the sea slapping against the shore. There wasn't a sound. Not a single squawk. Even seagulls didn't seem to know that the island existed.

"I'll tell you something else," Lauren said. "This has got to be the only place in Scotland that's not swarming with midges."

"What's that?" Hugh was pointing further to the left.

"A broken crate or something," Mike suggested.

Lauren went over to the weathered pieces of wood and wire. "I used to keep rabbits," she said, clearly upset. "That's what this is – or was. An old rabbit hutch – or maybe a guinea pig run."

Daniel never said much at the best of times. His stammer didn't help. And he didn't crowd round the latest mystery with the others. Instead, with his phone in his hand, he carried on walking, continuing the curve formed by the chain, skeletons and hutch. Every twenty paces or so, he made another discovery. First the remains of more creatures. Then some small wooden boxes, each with a wire mesh window and stuffed with something that looked like cotton wool. Next a sturdy rope attached to a peg driven into the ground. Sometimes Daniel's finds were in a dip, sometimes on a hump, but he realized that they were all leading him in a circle back to the metal chain.

Before he got that far, though, he froze.

Looking up at him, Annie called out, "What's up?"

Daniel simply pointed at the ground.

The other four dashed towards him.

When she got there, Lauren clasped her hands to her face and gulped.

This time, no one squatted down by the bones. They just stared until Hugh said, "I don't know, but that looks like…"

"What?" Mike asked.

"It looks human to me."

There was a chain and bracelet around what had been a leg.

"But it's so small," Lauren whispered. "Don't tell me it's a…"

Hugh took her arm. "Yes. I think it's a kid. I mean, a child."

"It's in a ring," said Daniel.

Hugh gazed at his brother. "What do you mean?"

"All these things – the skeletons and other stuff. They're in a circle."

Hugh scanned the scene. "You know, you might be right. Animals – and maybe even a little kid – tied up in a circle. We'd need to see it from the air to be sure."

Mike seemed to be fascinated by it all, but he was still fooling around. "Call for the family helicopter," he said with a smile. "I bet you've got one. Or two."

Daniel knew that Mike wasn't being spiteful. After all, he could see that Mike had fallen for his sister in a big way. But it was clear to Daniel that Mike had a problem. He probably wasn't jealous of their wealth, but maybe he felt sore about the gap between their lifestyle and his.

Annie was looking serious. "If all this stuff is in a ring, it makes you wonder what's in the middle, doesn't it?"

"Good point," Hugh muttered.

Daniel lingered by the skeleton for a moment before he followed the others to the centre of the circle.

There were two rusted metal cylinders by a hole in the patchy grass. Both were split open. The bigger one was about the size of a scuba diver's oxygen tank. Something had made it burst apart violently. The smaller canister had also been mangled. Hugh bent down and picked it up. It was the same size and shape as a test tube. He fingered it and said, "It's pretty old. Looks like a spent rifle cartridge, only bigger."

Annie took it from him. "You mean, it had an explosive in it?"

"Like a firework, yes."

"That's nice," Mike said. "Someone treated the animals to a firework display."

Hugh ignored him. "I don't know why, but I think it was made to blow up inside the other one."

Daniel kept his thoughts to himself. But he

realized that Annie, Hugh and Lauren were at different points on the scale from uneasy to afraid. Mike was simply curious and eager to explore.

Annie put the cartridge down. "That'd scatter whatever was in the big cylinder all over the place."

Lauren's voice was quiet and quaking. "All over the animals."

Hugh took both of her hands gently in his. "We don't even know if they were here when it went off," he said. "Or if they were alive at the time."

"I bet they were." Mike seemed to be the only one who hadn't realized that Hugh was trying to make Lauren feel better.

"Thanks for that, Mike." Hugh's voice dripped with sarcasm. "We'd better get back—"

Mike cut him short. "We can't stop now. We've got to get to the bottom of it. If we leave, we'll never know what this is all about. And it'll drive us mad wondering."

Daniel's instinct told him to turn round right

now, go back to the boat and get away. But even he was getting sucked into the mystery.

"Okay. Let's keep to the plan and head inland." Using his hand to shade his eyes, Hugh peered into the distance. "You know, I think there's something over there. Must be about the middle of the island. See?"

The haze played tricks on their vision.

"It's just a tree, isn't it?"

"Maybe. But…next to it?"

Mike took off. "One sure way to find out."

There were no paths to guide them, so they made their best guess and picked their way across the landscape. Daniel lagged behind, still fiddling with his mobile.

After a few minutes he waved it in the air and called out, "Annie! Can you call Mum and D-Dad?"

"Why?"

"Because I want to speak to them."

"You call them, then."

"I can't get a signal."

They all ground to a halt and reached into their pockets. Apart from Mike, they all had phones with loads of other functions. Daniel's played music files and doubled as a camera. Annie's had an internet connection. But none of them could raise a signal.

"Ha," Mike cried. "You can watch *Jurassic Park* or whatever on your mobiles, but they won't make a call."

"Will yours?"

Mike glanced down at his vacant screen. "No."

"I can't get an e-mail connection either," said Annie.

"Well, that's it." Hugh let out a groan. "We're on our own. Cut off."

"Unless we go back to the boat and use the radio," said Daniel.

"But we're not going back," Mike replied. "Not yet."

"He's right though," Annie said. "The radio's always there if we get into trouble."

Daniel wasn't so sure. The problem, he thought, was that they were already in trouble.

4

Daniel was good at figuring things out. Maybe it was because he did more listening and thinking than talking. His mind turned to that satellite image of nothing but sea. It wasn't a mistake, he was sure. Someone must be making it appear that this island didn't exist. And their mobile phones had gone silent. Was that deliberate as well? Or was the island simply too far from civilization and the nearest radio mast?

A waist-high rock poked up out of the earth. One side was covered in soil, grass and gorse. No bees foraged among the hardy yellow flowers. There were no spiders lurking in the cracks in the bare rock. Only patches of orange lichen clung to the rough surface. Beyond it, the ground sloped down into a hollow. And built into it was their next discovery.

It was a series of five wooden stalls. They were too small for horses, too large for rabbits. They had probably been constructed for keeping farm animals like sheep or pigs. Rain had decayed most of the planks near the bottom of the pens. The rest had been blasted smooth by wind and salt water. The iron locks were clogged with rust. Obviously, the stables had not been used for years, possibly decades.

Hugh looked around and shook his head. "You know, I think these things have been put in dips so you can't see them – until you're right on top of them. All very hush-hush."

"Great," Mike replied. "That means we might find lots more stuff."

Annie nodded. "There should be a house if someone lived here – and everything says someone did."

Hugh agreed. "A bleak place to live but...good point. Let's carry on and see." He put his arm round Lauren's narrow waist.

Before they set off again, Daniel decided to test them. "Which way's back to the boat?"

"That way." Lauren and Annie both pointed at the same time and in roughly the same direction.

"I hope you're not thinking of going back on your own," Hugh said, playing the protective older brother.

"No. I just think we ought to keep track of where it is." After a fit of violent coughing, Daniel bent down and picked up a small glass tube and plunger from outside the first pen. A long metal needle had been attached but it had decayed to little more than a thin brown stain on the rock.

"That's a syringe, Daniel. Don't…"

He dropped it as if it were red-hot.

Annie took a swig from her bottle of water and then handed it to Mike. As she did so, a gorse bush caught her eye. "Just a second." Going over to it, she bent down and picked up a glove that had lodged there. It wasn't an ordinary glove. For one thing, it was far thicker than normal. "It's rubber, I think. A bit cracked but still in one piece."

Hugh examined it. "Yes. Leather would've rotted away. As gloves go, it's heavy-duty."

"But what's it doing here?" Lauren asked. "And what was it used for?"

"Handling hippos?" Annie suggested with a grin. She let it fall and then flapped the bottom of her T-shirt to cool herself. "Phew. It's hot."

Mike nodded. "Global warming reaches Scotland at last."

"Look," Daniel said, pointing a short way ahead.

It was a large sheet of corrugated iron. "I'll tell you what'll be under this," Hugh said, kneeling beside it. "Snails and woodlice hiding from the sun. Maybe a frog or two as well."

"There won't be anything," Daniel replied quietly.

Hugh put both sets of fingertips underneath it and lifted, turning it over. Immediately, he looked up at Daniel. "Back home in the garden, this would be choked with creepy-crawlies. How did you know?"

"It's a d-dead island."

For a moment, the others gazed at Daniel in silence. Lauren trembled.

It was Annie who broke the spell. She put a hand to her brow to shield her eyes. "There *is* a tree ahead."

Still holding his useless mobile, Daniel followed her gaze. "Was," he muttered. "It's d-dead."

"And I can see a wiggly roof," Lauren said.

Touching the corrugated sheet with her foot, she added, "Just like this."

Mike nodded. "Yeah. It's your house, Annie. The one you said had to be here somewhere."

Hugh was back on his feet. "More like a rough-and-ready cottage. I can only see the roof. Must be low, built in a hole."

Annie glanced at him. "So it can't be seen from the sea."

"Exactly. And the wind's blown this chunk of roof off. An island like this will get plenty of wind. That's probably why the tree gave up the ghost."

"What are we waiting for?" Mike asked, heading straight for the concealed building. "Maybe it's a shop. I could murder an ice lolly."

"And I could murder you," Hugh replied.

Daniel watched Annie break into a smile. No doubt she guessed that their big brother had a sneaking regard for Mike and his daredevil attitude, despite the constant sparring. She was probably right.

She raced after Mike, grabbed both of his shoulders with her hands and jumped onto his back. "Yep," she shouted. "I can see from up here. Definitely a bungalow. A big one at that."

5

The shadow of the dead tree on the parched grass was a sharp black silhouette, as solid as the real thing. And it pointed towards the stone cottage with its low roof of corrugated iron. The building seemed to be squatting in the dip. There was a central square unit and four wings coming out from it, one at each corner.

At the end of the nearest wing there was a short blackened chimney, but no smoke rose from it. Several stones were missing from the walls underneath. They hadn't simply fallen out, because the gaps were in a regular pattern. The arrangement seemed to have been designed to draw air in or let it out. For some reason, Daniel shuddered when he saw it.

In several places, the bungalow's roof had been yanked off. Beyond the main block, there was a separate small building that looked like an outside toilet. The whole place had none of the niceties of a normal house. No garden. No yard. No drive. Nothing painted or colourful. It had clearly been abandoned.

"I'll tell you what's strange," Lauren said. "Not many windows, are there?"

"Come on." Annie went down into the hollow, heading for the wide front door. "I've got a feeling this is where we get some explanations."

"And something for a headache would be good," Hugh added with a pained expression.

Daniel said nervously, "Why d-don't we just walk round it?"

Mike shrugged. "Good idea. Check it out first." He led the way to the right.

Daniel wanted to walk around it and then leave. He hadn't meant they should walk around and then go in.

Part of the wall of the furthest wing had collapsed. Beyond the pile of fallen stone were a bedroom and a tiny kitchen. The lino on the floor of the kitchen was torn and curled at the edges. It had also lost its colour to years of sunlight and rain. In the corner, there was a camping gas cylinder attached to an antique cooker.

Lauren said, "They weren't holiday apartments, were they?"

"No," Mike replied with a laugh. "Who'd want to spend a holiday here? Nothing to do."

"There's loads," said Hugh. "Boating, fishing, and getting away from it all. Anyway, it hasn't been used for ages."

But strangely the cottage had not been taken over by nature. No plants or shrubs crawled over it. There weren't any roots undermining the walls. And the only tree nearby was dead.

"We could get in here," said Mike, pointing to the hole in the wall.

"Yeah," Hugh replied. "And the rest might cave in on us."

"I'm not clambering over that," Lauren said. "There's a perfectly good front door."

Mike shrugged. "Okay. Let's carry on."

Just beyond the smashed wall was a windowless outbuilding about the size of a shed. Like the bungalow itself, it was made of stone. To the side was a large tank for collecting rainwater.

"A shower block?" Annie guessed.

Mike yanked on the wooden door and at once it

fell off its rusted hinges. He jumped back to avoid it landing on his foot.

They all peered inside. It was some sort of storeroom. There were two corroded air cylinders, a butane gas canister, a paraffin can, lots of bottles of bleach, and many drums that had once contained various chemicals. On two of the drums, large yellow letters in a green shield spelled *BP*.

"The logo's ancient, but it's petrol," Hugh said, picking up one of the large containers and shaking it. "Or was. There's hardly anything left. I guess it was for boats."

Annie looked confused. "Why did they lug it all the way here, then?"

"Yeah," Mike added. "Even I know boats are kept on water."

Lauren wiped a finger across one of the cylinders. "Where are the cobwebs?" she said. "There should be lots. There's not even one!"

Daniel was sure he was looking at something

important. Bleach, chemicals he hadn't heard of, fuel, and an air supply. Along with everything else he'd seen on the island, the storeroom was a vital piece of an incomplete puzzle.

Mike turned to leave. "Let's carry on round."

The final wing had a large door and there were vertical bars instead of glass in the windows. Through the bars they could see rows and rows of cages and a concrete floor covered with shrivelled straw. A fishing rod lay along one wall, resting on a couple of rusty nails. Loops of rope were hanging from large hooks that had been driven into the walls.

"It's for keeping animals," said Hugh. "Lots of them."

Lauren screwed up her face. "Horrible."

"It's just a farm, isn't it?" Annie said. "A few chickens, rabbits, a cow, and some sheep maybe."

Daniel didn't believe her simple explanation. Neither did the others.

Mike was shaking his head. "It's a weird farm that

takes its animals across the island, pegs them out in a ring and gives them a firework display."

This time, it wasn't a joke.

They moved on, returning to the wide front door of the main building. Annie got there first. She grabbed the handle and cleared her throat. "Here we go," she said. "The moment of truth."

6

The door spoiled Annie's big moment. It didn't budge when she pushed. She applied both hands, then pushed and tugged again. Still, it refused to open. Surprised, she said, "I think it's locked."

Hugh turned towards Lauren. "Looks like we'll have to climb over—"

He was too late.

Mike slammed his foot into the wood and it burst open with a splintering sound.

Hugh sighed. "Nice work, Mike. Very subtle."

Mike bowed, waved both hands towards the gaping doorway and said, "After you, captain."

They filed into a large square room. It had no windows but the sunlight streaming through gaps in the ceiling let them see everything. It wasn't like a house or a farm. It reminded Mike of the shabby science laboratory in his school. In the middle, there was a big heavy bench with taps and sinks and old-style brown electrical sockets with round holes. Lying on top, there were two syringes like the one Daniel had found by the animal pens, another rubber glove, a scalpel and some small glass dishes. Built against the far wall was a row of glass-fronted cupboards that extended from waist height to the ceiling. Four interior doors led into the four wings and, on the left, there was an open trapdoor and a battered ladder that led down into a black hole.

Hugh peered into the void with a frown. "How can it go down? We're on solid rock."

Mike was standing behind him. "A dungeon carved out of stone. Good stuff. Let's see if there's a torch somewhere."

"You'd better find us a magic one," Hugh replied, "because I reckon the batteries will have gone flat by now."

All of them spread out around the room.

Lauren gasped as she neared one of the tall cupboards.

"What?" Hugh called.

"There's a gas mask in this one."

Hugh nodded. "Perhaps we're looking at something from the 1940s. You know, the war and all that. They might've been worried about being attacked by poison gas."

"Everything's really old but there's still no cobwebs," Lauren added suspiciously. "And what's that?"

Behind one of the glass panels was a big round bowl. In the centre was some sort of paddle connected to a frayed electrical cable. Clearly it had once rotated to stir whatever was in the bowl.

Mike covered up his unease with another wisecrack. "Was it used for making ice cream or candyfloss?"

"Somehow," Hugh replied, "I don't think so. Looks like a vat to me. The sort of thing you use to brew beer. Only it's too small for that."

"There are brown marks all over this bench," Annie said, rubbing at one patch with her finger. "What d'you reckon they are?"

It was Daniel who answered. "Bloodstains. Old ones." He sounded so certain that no one queried his opinion.

Annie grimaced and wiped her finger on her shorts.

Mike opened the door to the wing with the chimney and ventilation holes. All he saw was another door a couple of metres away. The set-up reminded him of an airlock in a submarine or a starship. The ones he'd seen in films at least. He pushed the second door open and immediately muttered, "Wow!"

"What now?"

"Come and look. It's…like an indoor barbecue."

It was darker in this wing, but shafts of sunlight stabbed the narrow space like sword blades. There were sacks of coal all along one side and an ironwork grill resting on a kiln at the end. Once, blazing coals had roasted whatever had been placed on the grill. The floor was littered with coal dust, ash and blackened scraps.

Drawing in a deep breath, Hugh said, "That's not a barbecue. It's a heavy-duty furnace." He bent down and picked up one of the black fragments, about the size of one of his fingers. "And that's a charred bone."

Lauren pulled a face.

Annie still seemed to be searching for an innocent

explanation. "This could be a farm type of thing as well, couldn't it? Animals kept outside, brought in here, killed and cooked. Not nice, I know, but that's what happens."

Hugh touched her bare arm and shook his head. "This goes way beyond cooking," he said. "Looks almost industrial. I think it's been used to burn animals' bodies. Completely."

Clearly upset, Lauren turned and walked out, back into the main room. Then she stopped dead. "What's that?" she cried.

The others joined her. "What?"

"There was a red light up there, above the way in."

A tiny plastic cube with a clear face had been positioned on the bare wall above the front door so it was behind them when they entered the cottage.

"It's not red," Annie said. But, as soon as she took a step towards it, it glowed like a traffic light on stop.

"I don't know what it is," said Mike, "but it looks new."

Straight away, Hugh was on edge. "It's a motion detector."

Mike stared at him. "What are you saying? That someone's watching us?"

"No. It's not a camera or a bug. It's like a burglar alarm. It senses movement."

"But where's the power to run it?" Annie asked.

"There's a wire. See?" Hugh pointed. "It's going up to the roof. I bet there's a solar panel charging its battery."

"Never mind how it's working," Lauren muttered. "Does it mean someone knows we're here?"

"I guess so," Hugh answered.

"Why would they monitor an old place like this?" Mike said.

Hugh kept his eyes on the motion detector. "Good question."

"Meaning you don't know."

"Maybe they aren't," Annie said. "Maybe it's just left over and nobody's taking any notice any more. We're the only people on the island."

Hugh shrugged. "It's the only modern thing we've seen since we left the boat."

"What are we going to do?" Lauren cried.

"Leave," Daniel muttered.

"No chance." Mike couldn't bear to pull out now. "Like Annie said, I bet no one's keeping an eye on it."

Lauren looked scared. "But…"

"We're not doing anything wrong," Annie reassured her. "This place is a wreck. Anyone could just walk in."

"Strictly speaking," Hugh replied, "I think we're trespassing."

Quoting the warning sign by the jetty, Daniel whispered, *"D-danger. Keep away from this island."*

"Yeah, but we're not hurting anyone," Annie said.

"Look, we've set it off now. We can't undo that,

so let's hurry up before the cops arrive." Then Mike added with a grin, "As if." He wandered towards the big bench. "We're looking for answers, remember. If it's worth protecting with a burglar alarm, it must be juicy." He looked at the electrical sockets and then turned towards the others. "Talking of power, how did these plugs work? Where'd the electricity come from?"

Hugh took a guess. "If there's a generator in the basement, that'd explain what the petrol's for. I bet the butane – camping gas – kept the cooker and things like that going."

Mike headed for the first door on the right of the main room. "Let's try in here."

But this time it was Daniel who stopped them in their tracks. He'd picked up a fragment of notepaper and was squinting at the faded writing. Then he read aloud, "*Observations after exposure trial. Pig 38, twenty yards from d-detonation...* I can't see any more. The rest is burned."

7

"Exposure trial?" Annie shrugged. "What does that mean? Sounds weird to me."

"Well, a detonation's what you do with explosives," Hugh told them. "Maybe it's something to do with those mangled canisters we found."

"The firework display," Mike said, still trying to lighten the mood. "So, someone was letting Pig 38 watch fireworks."

"From twenty yards," Annie added. "That's twenty metres in old-speak, isn't it?"

"A bit less."

Mike realized that Hugh wasn't showing off. He was just one of those boys who'd soaked up information and knew a lot of answers. Seriously boring, but suddenly useful.

Mike reached again for the door to the first wing, and led the way through.

There was a short passageway and two more doors, both on the left. Mike pushed open the first and peered inside. There was a toilet, a tin bath propped against the wall, a roll of Izal Medicated toilet paper, and a large basin with an enamel bowl. "It's a funny-looking loo."

Behind him, Annie and Hugh glanced in as well.

"It's a chemical toilet," Hugh said. "No sewer system on an island like this. And I bet the sink just drains outside."

Annie smiled. "No jacuzzi, then."

Behind the other door was a single bedroom with an abandoned mattress lying on a faded carpet. At the end of the short corridor was an area that had probably been used as a living room. Two old chairs, a cupboard and a table stood on its rough wooden floor.

"Where are the answers, then?" Lauren sounded frustrated. "This place has been cleared, hasn't it? More or less."

"More or less," Mike agreed. "But not everything's gone. There might still be a real giveaway lying around here somewhere."

"We've learned a lot already," Annie reminded them. "Like, they kept animals, gave them numbers, and incinerated them for some reason."

The discarded chairs had curved backs and round seats that had gone out of fashion ages ago. The wooden table had narrow drawers and thick curved legs that had once been painted light blue. Mike attempted to sit on one of the chairs, but it didn't take his weight and he jumped up at once. Instead, he toyed with an old-fashioned fork lying on the stained surface of the table.

Kneeling down, Annie moved a paraffin heater out of the way and opened the double doors of the cupboard. She peered inside and then plucked out three chunky white candles. "Look."

"Yeah!" Mike cried, dropping the heavy fork. "Now we can go down into the black hole."

"Not until you've worked out how to light them." Hugh turned to one side, sniffed and then sneezed.

Mike squatted beside Annie and together they felt around inside the cupboard. They came up with a pack of yellowed playing cards with pictures of sailors on them, a travelling chess set and an ashtray. Nothing else. No matches.

"Life was exciting here, wasn't it?" Mike said sarcastically. "No computer, no telly. Just cards and chess by the light of burning pigs."

Lauren scowled at him.

Hugh was beginning to look weary. "Give it a break, Mike."

The second apartment – the one with the broken wall – was also nearly bare. A tarnished pan was standing on the kitchen floor and there was a large round tin in the corner. Its plain bold lettering declared *6d Biscuit Assortment*, but it was empty apart from a few crumbs. Stacked on top were four white enamelled plates with blue rims. On the worktop there were five antique cans of food. Three contained baked beans. The smaller ones were labelled *Dried Whole Eggs* and *Lamb Tongues*.

Mike screwed up his face. "Lamb tongues! Eggs in a tin? Yuck."

"Powdered eggs," Hugh explained.

The drawer next to the cooker contained what they wanted. Annie put aside a tube of margarine that looked like toothpaste and picked up a small box of Scottish Bluebell matches.

Shaking it made a satisfying rattle. "A bit damp

but they look okay," she said, striking a match at the third attempt and lighting one of the candles. "Who's going down into the dungeon first?"

They all looked at Mike.

"You're the one who's gung-ho," said Hugh.

"Gung-ho? What does that mean?"

"A word invented especially for you. Reckless."

Mike laughed. "It's just that you like things safe and predictable. Boring. I like shocks and surprises. That's what keeps me going."

It was true. Ever since his mother had removed the stabilizers from his first bike, Mike had pushed himself and taken risks. He was attracted to the unknown lurking round the next corner. Or in a dark basement.

Mike headed back into the main room.

"I d-don't think it's a good idea," Daniel said.

"Why? Do you want to go first?" Mike asked him.

"No. I d-didn't mean... Nothing. You won't

listen to me." He put his hand on his neck as if his throat were sore.

Mike was about to step on the ladder, holding on to the wood and a lit candle at the same time, when he heard a familiar noise.

All five of them looked up, but the hole in the roof revealed only sky.

"It's a plane."

Mike was pleased to be able to correct Hugh for a change. "No. A helicopter." He paused before adding, "It'll be your mum and dad coming for you."

His joke fell flat. They listened for a few seconds more as the rotors beat the air louder and louder.

"It's coming this way," said Annie.

Mike nodded. "It's flying low."

Mike wasn't sure whether they should rush out to see it or not. After all, they had broken into the old cottage. Hugh was probably right when he said they were trespassing. Perhaps they shouldn't show themselves to the pilot. But curiosity got the better of him. Blowing the candle out and putting it down on the floor, he made for the door. The others followed him.

Shielding their eyes from the sun, they watched the helicopter getting closer. They couldn't make out the pilot or any passengers. Soon, the chopper was hovering over their heads, its downdraught ruffling their hair and cooling their skin. It made no attempt to land. After a few moments, it set off again. They watched it circling the island, apparently following the coastline. When it reached the spot where they had left their boat, it swooped low. Then it backed away.

Making them jump with shock, it let loose some sort of missile that flew downwards, out of sight, and exploded. A flame shot up briefly above the rocky landscape and then died down again. Grey smoke drifted lazily into the air as the helicopter circled the area twice and then headed swiftly back towards the mainland, its characteristic throbbing becoming gradually fainter.

"What happened?" Annie exclaimed.

Hugh looked stunned. "I think they just blew our boat up."

8

Fearing the worst, they sprinted back across the island, making for the column of smoke.

They came to a sudden halt on the rocks above the jetty. But there was no jetty any more. There was no boat either. Fragments of the motor launch had been scattered all over the shore, littering the rocks. Some pieces were floating on the gently rolling waves, some were sinking. Some larger parts were blackened by flame, others had been reduced to dust that hung in the air. The fuel had ignited and blasted the engine apart.

They all stood open-mouthed and unable to speak.

Mike found his voice first. "What have we done to deserve that?"

"How are we going to get off the island now?" Daniel gasped.

Shaken out of his silence, Hugh muttered, "We're not just stranded. Our food's gone as well."

"And the radio," Daniel added.

"This has got something to do with that motion detector, hasn't it?" Annie said. "Someone knows we're here and doesn't want us to leave."

"D-didn't you see what type of helicopter it was?"

"How do you mean?"

"I think it was the RAF," Daniel answered. "The RAF's stranded us here!"

For a while, they were struck dumb again. Then Mike blurted out, "But they're supposed to be on our side."

"Not here, they're not."

"What are you saying, Daniel?"

"We're the enemy now. That's what the island's d-done to us. Turned us into the enemy."

Daniel checked his mobile phone but it still wasn't responding. He wasn't surprised. He no longer thought it was because they were too remote. If the authorities could bomb their boat and interfere with satellite maps of the area, surely they could jam telephone network signals as well. The thought made him shiver.

Lauren was terrified. "Who got us into this?" she shouted, staring at Mike.

"We all did," Annie replied. "Not just Mike."

"What are we going to do?" Lauren asked, on the edge of panic.

"I can't believe what's just happened but…" Hugh

put his hands on Lauren's shoulders. "It's true. We all agreed to land here – apart from Daniel."

Lauren shrugged him off. "So what are we going to do?" she repeated.

It was plain that Hugh was struggling to cope, but he was doing the best he could, because he thought the oldest should show courage and leadership. "We've got to stop arguing and work together."

Lauren shook her head. "But how do we get home?"

"Well, standing here isn't going to bring the boat back," Annie said.

"Yeah," Mike agreed. "Let's carry on in the house. If we get to the bottom of what's going on, maybe—"

"That's pathetic," Lauren snapped. "What if they shoot *us* next time?"

Hugh tried to calm her down. "They won't. We'll be okay. Someone'll come."

"Someone with guns."

"No." Hugh held her hand this time. "I mean, someone'll come to rescue us." He paused for a moment and then said, "That's it! Mum and Dad will come. As soon as they realize they've lost contact, they'll come for us."

"How will they find us?" said Mike. "This island doesn't exist, remember?"

Annie nodded. "He's right, Hugh. It's up to us to sort ourselves out now."

"By doing what?" Lauren demanded.

Hugh seemed dazed; he didn't have any more answers. "I still can't believe this has happened."

Annie gazed at the remains of their boat. "Well, we can't make it *un*happen. Maybe Mike's got a point. Maybe we can find something to help back at the house. Like an old radio."

Mike agreed. "We might strike it lucky down in the dungeon."

"There's something else," Daniel added.

"What?"

"We haven't been all round the island. There might be another boat somewhere."

At once, Hugh looked relieved. "Yeah. That's another way forward."

Lauren's temper seemed to improve as well. She was more frightened than furious. "All right. Let's go back."

Along with Annie and Lauren, Daniel was sitting on the heavy horsehair mattress that they'd dragged into the central room. Mike was walking restlessly round and round the big bench, while Hugh perched on it, dangling his legs. "Let's come up with priorities first," he suggested.

Lauren muttered, "Staying alive." She had lost the ability to speak normally. Everything came out as a frantic shout or a sullen whisper.

"Well, not a bad place to start."

"Yeah," Mike agreed. "I'm hungry and all we've got is powdered eggs, lambs' tongues, and three cans of beans from the dawn of time."

"The beans'll be all right," Annie replied. "They last for ever, don't they?"

"What's their use-by date?"

"No chance," Annie answered. "They didn't have use-by dates, best-befores or anything else when these beans got baked."

"Even if they're all right," said Mike, "how long can five of us live on three cans of beans?"

Hugh said, "Eating isn't the main problem."

"What is, then?"

"They say you can go three minutes without air, three days without water, and three weeks without food. There's plenty of air, so the most important thing's water, not food. Anyway, I saw a fishing rod in the bit where they kept animals, so we can catch something to eat."

Lauren threatened to explode again. "You're all talking like we're going to be here for ages!" she exclaimed. "We've got to get away, not work out how to stay!"

Gently, Hugh said, "We can't get away right now."

"We're going to find a radio or a boat," she insisted. "That's what we said."

Hugh nodded. "Sure."

"I want to find out what's going on as well." Mike glanced at the black hole and the candles. "I want to know why the RAF stopped us leaving. That's high on my list."

"Why don't we split up?" Hugh said. "Lauren – you and Daniel could check out the rest of the island."

"And hide if you hear a helicopter coming," Annie put in.

"The rest of us can explore the water supply and cellar."

Daniel agreed. He knew that Lauren would too. She would have preferred to stay with Hugh, but not if it meant going down into a grotty hole in the ground. She wasn't cut out for roughing it. Searching the coast for a boat would seem like a good deal in comparison.

"Okay. Let's get going," said Lauren. "I don't want to be here a minute longer than I have to be." She got up and looked around.

"What are you after?" Hugh asked.

"A drink. I'm thirsty."

He shrugged. "Sorry. We finished the bottles of water."

"Great," Lauren muttered. "Come on, Daniel. We need a boat. And fast."

9

Behind the cottage, Mike jumped up and grabbed the lip of the water tank. Heaving with his arms and scrabbling with his feet, he pulled himself up until his chin was level with the top of the container, and looked inside. Then he let go and landed with a thud on the thin layer of soil.

"Well?" Hugh prompted.

"Yeah. There's quite a bit left. About half full."

"That means it's about half empty," said Hugh. "But is it clean?"

Annie snorted. "I don't think he carried out the full range of purity tests while he was hanging in mid-air."

"Did it look clean?" Hugh asked.

"I suppose so. It was water-coloured, not black."

"I mean, are there any animals in it? Like drowned rats or birds."

"No," Mike answered. "Just a hippo taking a bath."

Hugh grimaced. "This could be a matter of life and death, you know."

"Sorry, sir." Then he winked at Annie as if he'd just been hauled in front of the head teacher for being naughty. "I'll try to behave better in future."

Despite their situation, Annie smiled.

That's why Mike liked her. Because she wasn't

like Hugh and his model girlfriend. Annie had spirit and a belief that everything would turn out all right in the end.

Turning his back on them, Hugh followed the pipe from the tank as it led back to the house. It went directly into a box attached to the base of the wall. Squinting at the worn writing printed on the side, Hugh said, "I think it's a filter unit. The stuff coming out of the taps will be filtered rainwater. Stagnant, but it might be okay. If all else fails, we could risk drinking it, but we'll have to run it a while to clear the pipes out."

Behind him, Mike said, "You can try it first."

"Okay. If you go down the cellar first."

Mike's feet had disappeared into the hole. Annie handed him a lit candle. "Be careful," she said.

"Test each rung before you put your weight on it," Hugh advised. "The wood might be rotten."

"Ah, I didn't know you cared," Mike replied, as he looked down.

Hugh coughed loudly. "If you fall down and kill yourself, it's a terrible waste of a candle."

Mike smiled. "You love me really."

"Just get on with it, you two," Annie cried. "Or I'm off to join Daniel and Lauren."

The steps of the ladder seemed solid enough, so Mike carried on down. Soon, only his shoulders and head poked above the floor. He still couldn't see where he was going or how far he had to go. "This candle's not exactly high-powered, is it?"

Annie grabbed another one. "I'll follow you."

"Not till he gets to the bottom," Hugh warned. "We don't know how much weight the ladder will take."

"He's right," Mike agreed. "One guinea pig at a time."

"Actually," Hugh said, "they used a canary – not a guinea pig – to check if the air was breathable down a mine."

Before his head disappeared, Mike replied, "Canary, guinea pig, poor kid. It's all the same."

Mike got the impression that the ground wasn't far below. Maybe it was the way his voice echoed. Maybe it was because the ladder wasn't wobbling much. He also had the feeling that he wasn't descending into some huge underground cavern.

Looking up, he could see Annie's concerned face. "There's a trapdoor dangling down. If someone took the ladder away, it'd close the hole up, I think." He held out the candle to get a better look. "It's like a submarine door. You know, with a little wheel instead of a handle."

Hugh's head appeared above him. "Sounds like it's a heavy-duty seal, making it airtight down there for some reason."

"I'm carrying on."

"Are you at the bottom?"

Mike let out a shriek. "I've just stepped on a dead body!"

"What?" the other two shouted down at the same time.

Mike laughed. "Not really." He hesitated and added, "Just touched the floor. It's rock or something. More or less flat."

"When I get down there," Hugh called, "there *is* going to be a dead body. Yours."

Above Mike, Annie's face seemed to be framed in a skylight. "It's all right down here," he called up to her, "but I could use a bit more candle power."

"I'm coming…"

Hugh interrupted his sister. "Just look around first, Mike. Is it safe? What's down there?"

"I can't see much. It's square, about ten paces wide. There's an old table and chairs." They were foldable, probably originally intended for camping. Holding out his candle, Mike made his way slowly to the far wall. It was rough rock. In front of it were four cabinets. "There's some lockers as well – like at school – and more gas cylinders. Hang on. There's…"

"What?" Annie asked from above.

Propped against the wall were two identical cases. Mike put the candle down on the floor and grabbed one of them with both hands. He peered at the label on top. "More old stuff," he called out. "Like a small suitcase, but it says *Survival Kit* on it."

"Could be useful," said Hugh. "Anything else? Like a radio?"

When Mike picked up the candle, the light caught a scrap of paper on the floor. He bent down, held the flame close to it, and read out, "*Animal Inventory.* There's a date. Something of March, 1947. Then it's a list of animals with numbers. Sheep, pigs, rabbits, rats, dogs, cats, monkeys..."

"Monkeys?" Hugh's voice seemed to boom down into the small cellar room.

"Yeah."

Hugh breathed a sigh of relief. "Those bones weren't a baby, then. I bet it was a monkey skeleton."

"Phew," Annie muttered.

"But it's weird. You don't get a lot of monkeys on your average farm," Hugh added.

Mike put the piece of paper on the table. "No radio as far as I can see, but there's some sort of engine in the corner." He kneeled down and examined it. "It's ancient."

"Has it got a starter handle?" Hugh asked.

"Maybe. There's a long pole thing at the front. Oh, there's a can of petrol as well."

"Yes!" Hugh said. "That's a generator. We might be able to get it going if it's got petrol. Don't put the candle near the petrol can."

"A good job you told me," Mike replied, pretending to be insulted. "I was about to open the can and stick the flame in to see if there's any left."

"There's a bit more petrol outside in the shelter," Hugh said. "Or it might run on paraffin at a push."

"I'm coming down," Annie announced.

As Annie climbed down, her body blocked the weak sunlight penetrating the strange cellar through the hatch. When she reached the bottom, the faint shaft of sunshine returned and the second candle boosted the level of light.

Mike spread out his arms. "Welcome to my palace."

"The air's a bit stale... Oh, look." She pointed to the other side of the underground den. "Three more mattresses."

Mike nodded. "Bed and breakfast. Without the breakfast."

Another dark shadow engulfed them while Hugh came down through the hole. Landing on the rock floor, he said, "Looks like a survival capsule to me."

"Is that a posh name for a hideout?"

Hugh didn't answer.

Mike went to the far corner and peered into another chemical toilet. It was stained intense blue where the disinfectant had long since evaporated.

Holding the last candle, Hugh went along the row of lockers, yanking on each door. The third one yielded to his tugging. He let out a gasp as the door flew open and something about the size of a man fell out.

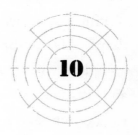

10

The thing flopped onto the ground in a crumpled mess and Annie screamed. In the days that he'd known her, Mike had not heard her do that before. She wasn't the sort of girl who screamed. Maybe the island was getting to her. Mike had to admit it was becoming more and more scary. He could understand a scream just slipping out.

"What is it?" Mike exclaimed, staring at the sinister shape on the floor.

"Looks like a spacesuit," Annie said, recovering from the shock.

Hugh kneeled down. "Yes. Something like that." He grappled with the rubber costume, complete with hood, gloves, transparent face shield and attached tubes. "It's all-over gear. Completely isolates whoever's wearing it."

"How do they breathe?" Mike asked.

Hugh shook one of the tubes. "This gets attached to an air cylinder, I think." He paused before adding, "That'd explain the tanks down here and the spares outside."

Annie grimaced. "But why? What was around here that meant they had to wear spacesuits?"

"Well, they weren't flying space missions in 1947 for sure, so I guess it's a chemical protection suit. That means there was some sort of poison on the island, I suppose."

"Let's hope *was* is right," Annie remarked. "It'd better not still be here."

"It was more than sixty years ago. All that wind, rain and sun will have broken it down or washed it away by now." Hugh stood up and looked into the open cabinet. There was another gas mask hanging on its back wall. Its blunt protruding nose that contained a filter to absorb poisonous gases made it look grotesque. "Think of the time. The 1940s. It's got to be something left over from the war," he said.

"So, this is an air-raid shelter?" said Annie.

"It fits. Maybe they were scared about a chemical weapon being dropped on them."

"No chance!" The force of Mike's reply nearly snuffed out his candle. "Why would anyone bomb an island stuck in the middle of nowhere?"

Hugh shrugged.

Annie froze to the spot.

"Annie?"

"I was thinking about that list of animals," she said. "Why import a load of animals? Maybe they were testing poisons on them, finding out what happened in case the Germans tried a gas attack or something. You can't really use people, so the animals copped it instead."

Hugh thumped his sister on the back. "Brilliant! They loaded whatever the poison was into that shell and detonated it on the other side of the island. The animals were put out in a ring and exposed to it. That's why Daniel's bit of paper talked about an exposure trial. Then they took them to the paddock to watch what happened. They'd bring them here afterwards – to do more tests and post-mortems maybe. And to burn them."

Annie nodded. "Makes sense." Then she mumbled to herself, "A horrible sort of sense."

"Someone had to do it, I guess," Hugh said. "To protect the people."

"But…" Mike didn't finish his sentence.

"What?"

"If that's it, why did the RAF blast our boat to bits?"

"I dread to think," Annie muttered.

Hugh let out a groan.

"What's up?" Annie asked him.

"You mean, apart from being stranded in a weird lab on a secret island?"

"Yes."

"Just my killer headache, that's all."

Annie looked sympathetically at her pale brother. "Maybe there's some aspirin in the survival kits."

"Did they have aspirin in those days?" Mike said.

"Yeah. I think it's been around for ages."

"Forget it," Hugh said. "It's only a headache. But, yes, let's take the survival kits upstairs when we go so we can have a good look."

Mike forced open the door to another locker. On its shelves was a collection of glass bottles. Each one had a label that read *Drinking Water*.

"Didn't know they had bottled water all those years ago."

"I don't suppose they did in the shops," Hugh replied. "But this is a survival capsule. They'd need water. It's something else to take up in case the stuff out of the taps is horrible."

"Look." Mike moved one of the bottles, took a small square of paper from underneath it and held it near the candle flame. "It's a photo. A woman – like an old film star. No one looks like this any more."

The woman was probably in her twenties, standing outside a tiny terraced house and smiling broadly.

"Is there anything on the back?"

Mike turned it over. The ink had faded but the fancy handwriting was just visible. *With love, Betty, 1946,* Hugh and Annie read over his shoulder.

"Maybe she's happy because the war's just ended."

Mike shrugged and slipped the black-and-white photograph into his pocket.

Hugh tried to prise open the doors of the other

two lockers with his fingertips but he failed. They were securely locked. "Let's find something to force them open."

"There's a strong-looking fork on the living-room table," Mike told him.

Hugh made for the ladder.

"Hang on a second. Leave us your candle," Annie said. "Stay at the top and we'll hand the survival kits and bottles of water up to you."

"Good thinking."

Hugh lifted all their trophies into the main room and then he went to find the fork. When he returned to the hole again, he lay on the floor and handed it down to Annie.

Straight away, she jammed it into the gap in the first locker. The fork was much bigger and sturdier than modern ones. It bent a little as she forced it back, but the thin metal casing of the cabinet buckled first. A gap opened between the door and the side panel, freeing the lock.

"What's inside?" asked Hugh, his head filling the square of light from the hatch.

Annie grabbed a large box from the bottom of the cabinet and pulled it out. Looking at the words on the top of the container, she read, "*Paragon First-Aid Outfit.*"

Reaching back inside, she removed a much smaller rectangular can from the shelf. "And a tin of boiled sweets," she said. "That's your headache and Mike's hunger taken care of."

"Is that all?" Hugh asked, plainly disappointed.

"Can't see anything else," Annie replied.

She forced the final locker open, revealing another chemical protection suit. Raising her arm, she felt around on the high shelf. "There's something here," she muttered. "What's this?"

Annie and Mike peered at the small shiny case that filled her palm and reflected the wavering candlelight. It was square in shape and thinner than a pack of cards. One corner was inscribed with the initials *JM*.

"I don't know," Annie said. "It might be silver." She struggled to push in the small clasp and then lift the lid. Inside, there were five scraggy cigarettes. "An old cigarette case," she said. "Yuck."

Losing interest, she put it down on the table.

To make sure they'd left nothing behind, Mike swept his hand over the shelf. And he felt something that was similar in size to the cigarette case but soft. A small notebook. He examined his find by the candle flame. There was a date printed on the cover: *1947*.

"A notebook!" he exclaimed. Flicking through the pages, he said, "There's some writing, but not a lot."

Annie sounded excited. "Let's go up and get a good look in decent light. This could be exactly what we need."

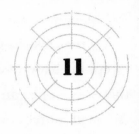

11

Daniel and Lauren had reached a point on the island that was exactly opposite the spot where they had moored their boat. The landscape had not changed at all and they'd seen nothing of interest. Certainly nothing that would get them off the island.

The ocean was an unbroken blue-grey. As far as Daniel could see, there was nothing out there.

No shipping. No helicopters. Not even a bird. Just a vast expanse of sea. Thinking about the position of the island, he said, "Canada's that way. Straight ahead. Greenland must be over there." He pointed to the right.

Lauren brushed some soil off the bottom of her trousers with her hand. Then she shook her head. "You know, I can't help feeling I'm about to wake up. All this is just…"

"A terrible d-dream?" Daniel suggested.

"Yes."

Daniel wasn't sure about Lauren. She'd been going out with Hugh for about eight months, but their relationship didn't seem special. They looked at ease with each other rather than excited to be together. Daniel suspected Hugh mainly liked Lauren for her looks and Lauren mainly liked Hugh for his family's lifestyle. She'd quickly become part of the background.

After less than a week, Daniel felt he knew Mike

much better. A strong character like Mike made an immediate impact. That was why Annie had kept him away from their parents. She knew they'd turn their noses up at Mike, while they were all in favour of Lauren. There was a huge divide between Hugh's classy girlfriend and Annie's new boyfriend. One was made for designer gear, and the other was never seen in anything but cheap, torn jeans. Mike would never become part of the background. He was too lively for that. His relationship with Annie already seemed special – awkward, fun-filled and crazy. And Daniel's parents would never approve.

Lauren stopped walking, pushed her blonde hair behind her ears and looked at Daniel. "Why didn't Claudia come with us? She never seems to join in, does she?"

At the mention of his other sister, Daniel dropped his gaze and stared at the rock under his feet. "She… er…likes her own space."

"Really? What does that mean?"

"Well, you've met her. And Hugh must've said something."

Lauren nodded. "About as much as you."

"You know she's adopted, d-don't you?"

"Yes. The three of you – Hugh, Annie and you – have got the same look, but not Claudia. Lighter skin. Not so...refined, if you know what I mean. Attractive in her own way. But that doesn't tell me why she doesn't join in."

Daniel began to walk along the coastline again. "She's all right really. Just d-does things her own way. She's a loner."

"I've seen that for myself, but it doesn't explain why, does it?"

Daniel didn't feel like saying any more. He shrugged. "She just d-doesn't fit in."

The sun was well past its highest point and cloud was now swelling on the horizon. Daniel didn't doubt that the sea would normally pound the rocky coast, but today it merely stroked the shoreline.

Lauren changed the subject. "What do you think's going on here?"

Daniel was surprised, not accustomed to someone older caring about his opinions. "I'm not sure."

"But what do you think?"

"I think someone was d-doing nasty animal experiments."

"I know they test drugs on animals but that's not what you're saying, is it?"

Daniel shook his head. He was about to say more when he spotted something on a feeble patch of grass and gorse. "Look."

They both squatted down by a man's brown leather shoe. It was very old-fashioned, heavy and badly worn.

"Who leaves one shoe behind?"

Lauren was speaking to herself really but Daniel answered anyway. "Someone in a hurry."

They stood up again and looked around. The shoreline dipped down so that the coast was out of their view. Without a word, they walked towards the lip of the rock. Looking over, they both gasped.

They were staring down at a narrow inlet that had once provided a tiny hidden harbour with space for one boat. Hardly anything was left. The harbour itself had been obliterated, possibly by a bomb. There must have been a boat there when it was destroyed because pieces of painted wood littered the inlet and a row of curved planks, like a giant's ribcage, poked out of the water.

"It looks just like our jetty," Lauren whispered, "after it was blown up."

There was a vague path leading down to the waterfront and, at the end of it, a sign. The board was still standing, suggesting that it had been put up after the place had been wrecked, but it was facing out to sea, so they couldn't read it from where they stood.

They glanced at each other, shrugged, and set off down the slope. Approaching the noticeboard, Lauren stooped down and picked up a piece of tarred timber. Erosion by wind and water had left it smooth to the touch. "It's from a boat, isn't it?"

Daniel nodded. "The keel." He swallowed before continuing. "It's just like what happened to ours. Only this was years ago."

Lauren agreed. "No plastic or fibreglass. Just wood."

Pushing aside some seaweed with his foot, Daniel revealed a large bone.

"Another animal or..." Lauren didn't want to finish her sentence.

"I d-don't know but..." Daniel shivered. "Maybe, when the boat got blasted, someone was on board."

Neither of them wanted to dwell on that horrible thought. They walked round to the front of the sign. The words of warning were still visible. Both Daniel and Lauren turned pale as they read the notice.

This island has been, and for the time being remains, quarantined. Keep away. Landing is strictly prohibited. By order of the Government.

"Quarantined!" Lauren muttered. "That means it's infected with something."

"We'd better go back and tell the others."

Lauren seemed to be spellbound by the warning sign. She was also trembling. "This is the island's front door, isn't it? We came in through the back door and missed the full health warning."

"If Mike had seen it, he would've still wanted to land."

"But he would've been outvoted."

Daniel was certain that Annie liked mystery as much as Mike. She liked to feel her heart racing. She would have voted to ignore the warning and explore the forbidden island too. He also knew that she believed every adventure would turn out okay in the end. "You and me versus Annie and Mike," he said. "Two all. It would've been d-down to Hugh."

Turning away, Daniel led the way back up the path, towards the stone cottage.

Lauren followed. "Hugh would've voted against. We'd have moved on."

Daniel nodded in agreement. "But we d-didn't. We're stuck here now."

12

"**I**nfected!" Annie exclaimed.

"Well," Lauren said, "that's what quarantine means, doesn't it? Isolating people to stop a germ spreading." She gulped down stale water from one of the old bottles.

"At least bugs don't last sixty years," Hugh chipped in.

Annie examined her brother's face. "Are you sure?"

"Yes." His answer was delivered with confidence but his expression hinted at doubt.

"So, the gas masks and all-over suits were to stop whoever was here from catching some sort of disease," Annie guessed. "And they used explosive shells to scatter the germs over experimental animals."

"Probably to find out what would happen if the bad guys dropped biological weapons on the country," said Hugh.

"Annie's spot on," Mike announced.

Surprised by his abrupt remark, they all turned towards Mike.

While they'd been talking, Mike had skimmed through the old notebook. "This book belongs to Jack MacLeod, whoever he is. Anyway, listen to this bit: *A small upright explosive rod in the centre of the munition tore the metal in a useful manner whilst burning as small an amount of Agent A as possible. Farm and experimental animals were also fastened at various distances and elevations to measure the extent of infection when exposed to the discharged agent."*

"Agent A," Daniel muttered.

"Do you know anything about it? Has anyone heard of it?" Hugh asked.

They all shook their heads.

Annie said, "Is there anything else about it in Jack's notebook?"

Mike didn't get on with books. He was more a doer than a reader. He held it out to Annie. "I don't know. You look."

Lauren didn't wait for Annie to scan the scratchy writing. "No boat and no radio. Just someone's scribbling." Looking at Mike, she added, "You said we'd be better off if we found out what went on here, didn't you? Well, how does that help us get away?"

"Hey, don't take it out on me. At least we know what we're up against."

"We know why the RAF stopped us getting away," Daniel said. "They think Agent A's still around and they d-don't want us spreading it back home. That's why it's a d-dead island. No animals or insects. Agent A's still here."

They all stared silently at Daniel until Hugh asked Annie, "Is there anything about how long Agent A hangs around?"

Without looking up, she replied, "Not that I've seen yet. Maybe they didn't know back then."

"The people who put that sign up at the harbour – the Government – knew," Lauren said. "They think you can still catch it."

"But what is Agent A?" said Hugh. "What does it do?"

"If my phone worked," Annie said, "I could look it up on the web. But…" She shrugged. "It doesn't. And no one even knows about this island, so I don't suppose Agent A will be splashed all over the internet."

Mike was delving into the first-aid kit, extracting bandages, cotton wool, plasters, a thermometer, Epsom salts, an ancient tin of Germolene antiseptic cream, and a small tube that looked like glue but was labelled *Anti-gas Ointment*.

Hugh studied the tube and said, "That'll be for burns if you get nerve gas on your skin, or that sort of thing. Standard issue in the war."

Mike taunted him. "Remember it well, do you?"

"I thought you were finding me some aspirin for my headache."

"It'll take more than aspirin to fix a brain like yours." Mike hesitated before adding sympathetically, "Only kidding. Sorry. I can see you're feeling rough." He examined a small bottle of tablets and then handed it to Hugh. "Try them. It says *Parkinson's Sugar-Coated Headache Pills*. Probably iffy but you never know."

Annie looked up again from the notebook. "Jack MacLeod and Betty – the woman in the photograph

– were an item," she reported. "He keeps mentioning her. How much he's missing her, how he looks at her picture whenever he can."

"What about Agent A, though?"

"Oh, no!" Annie groaned. "Listen: *This strain of anthrax was originally isolated from a diseased cow near Oxford in 1935. We call it Agent A and its properties are ideal. It grows well in a vat and it is highly resistant to decomposition. It survives for decades in soil. On being breathed in, eaten or absorbed into a cut in the skin, it reactivates itself and multiplies in the host most rapidly. It causes an invariably fatal respiratory infection."*

There were several seconds of stillness before Mike said, "I don't like the sound of that." This time, his voice was not playful.

"A is for anthrax," Hugh muttered.

"What's anthrax?" asked Mike.

"It's a bacterium," Hugh answered. "A germ. But it's been used deliberately to kill people. Like, anthrax spores have been sent through the post in letters."

"Is that germ warfare, then?"

Hugh nodded. "Exactly."

"There's more," Annie told them. "*The Nazi threat has now passed and Mr. Churchill is no longer considering the release of anthrax on German soil...*"

Hugh looked astounded. "You mean, we were developing it to attack Germany? But I thought we'd be doing all this for defence."

Mike didn't get on with history either. He was puzzled. "So, we were making anthrax bombs. But we were the good guys in the war, weren't we?"

"Obviously, the Germans surrendered before we let it loose," Annie said. "But the work carried on after that. *Our experiments are now coming to an end. It is not soon enough. I long to be back in Betty's arms. Before we leave, we are to complete the current sequence of trials with a new strain of anthrax. Boxes containing cotton wool will be located around the site to capture and count the anthrax spores that remain active after detonation. Then we will clear the island of any evidence of our research."*

"Huh," Mike grunted. "Leaving notes is a funny way to strip the place of evidence."

Hugh glanced around. "Most of their stuff's gone, but not everything. I reckon they left in a hurry before they finished clearing up."

"Or maybe Jack wanted someone to find the notebook – to know what they'd been d-doing," Daniel suggested.

"And there's a bombed boat in the harbour," Lauren added. "That means they weren't supposed to leave, doesn't it?"

Daniel nodded. "My guess is something went wrong. Maybe they got infected with Agent A. I d-don't know, but it looks like they made a run for it. Then someone blew them up before they got away."

"To stop the germ escaping?" Lauren said.

"Maybe. It fits with what we know."

Mike rated Daniel. He was the youngest, but there was something about him. He was quiet but, when he did say something, it was well thought out. If Daniel had conjured up an explanation, Mike was inclined to believe him.

"It fits politics as well," Annie added. "The Government wouldn't want to admit they were making anthrax bombs, so they blew Jack and his mates away to make sure nobody found out."

"And we're getting the same treatment," said Daniel.

"What? Because we're infected, you mean?" Lauren asked. "Or because we're finding out what happened here?"

"It's only a theory," Hugh pointed out, probably to comfort his girlfriend. "You could come up with other explanations. They could've been winding up the operation when one of them refuelled their boat and got careless. Maybe he was smoking and set fire to the petrol. Blew the boat up by accident."

Mike peered at him and said, "Do you believe that?"

"Well..."

"No, he doesn't." Lauren put her head in her hands. "It's all too horrible. We're in deep trouble, aren't we? What if we *are* infected? What if that's why you're feeling bad, Hugh? What's going to happen to us?"

Mike looked at the others. None of them seemed willing to answer.

13

The survival kits were a big disappointment. They contained a blanket, a penknife, a fire-lighting flint, a needle and thread, some safety pins, a candle and a pack of matches, a whistle, a bottle of water, and a waterproof overall.

"A working mobile would trump this lot," Hugh muttered. He looked in a bad way now, as if someone had his head in a vice. Obviously, the ancient pills had done nothing to ease his throbbing head and he was getting worse. Even so, he was making an effort to look calm and confident for the sake of the others, especially Lauren. He took a deep breath. "Mike, you're into camping. You try and get the gas cooker going."

Mike nodded. "If we had adults here, they'd fix everything by putting the kettle on and making a nice cup of tea."

Trapped on a poisoned island, clearly feeling lousy, Hugh laughed at one of Mike's wisecracks. It wasn't very funny but perhaps he laughed to release a bit of tension. "Pity we haven't got a tea bag," he added.

"Or a kettle."

"Well, see if you can get the cooker going anyway. If we're going to risk the baked beans, it'd be safer if we boiled them up first. And when we've run out of bottled water, we can boil the stuff out of the taps as well." He glanced at his watch. "It'll be dark in a few hours, so I'll try and get the generator up and running."

Lauren looked fearfully through the roof at the sunset.

"Are you sure you're up to it?" Annie asked Hugh.

"Sure," he said, trying to stay chirpy. "Nothing to worry about. We've got everything under control and it's about now that Mum and Dad'll start getting anxious. When they can't get through to us, they'll phone the coastguard. Then there'll be a search. That means we should take it in turns to stay up and keep watch."

"Why don't we light a big bonfire?" Mike suggested.

"Because it might attract the attention of that helicopter."

"Perhaps whoever's on watch should take the fishing rod and catch some mackerel while they're at it," Annie said. "Not a bad idea to keep the food stocks up, just in case."

"In case of what?" Lauren asked.

Annie shrugged. "In case we're here longer than we'd like. In case the coastguard doesn't find us straight away, I suppose."

Lauren muttered, "We've already been here longer than we'd like. We should be doing something to escape."

"Like?"

"Building a raft."

Hugh pulled a face. "That's harder than it sounds, Lauren. A raft that'll cope with five people and the sea is tricky."

"And dangerous," Annie said.

Lauren was clearly desperate. "It's dangerous here on land. We could pull the stables down, couldn't we? Plenty of wood there."

Hugh looked doubtful. "But how do we turn it into something that won't fall apart as soon as the waves get at it?"

Obviously Lauren had been thinking about it

because she answered straight away. "There's rope on the wall by those animal cages."

"It's an idea, but..." Hugh shook his head and then winced with pain. "Easier said than done. Let's keep it in reserve – in case the rescue services don't show up."

Mike thought Lauren should lay off pestering her boyfriend when he was feeling rotten. Less subtle than Hugh, he said, "Being trapped on dry land is better than drowning in a home-made boat. I'm all for adventure and risk, but not suicide."

There was a loud bang followed by an uneven chug and Hugh yelled. "Yes! We have lift-off."

The spluttering generator made the cottage lights flicker timidly into life. It also made Annie and Mike cheer.

"Old, but still working," Hugh shouted, his head rising up through the hole. "I don't know how long the petrol's going to last, though." With a groan, he dragged himself up and joined Annie, who was sitting on the lab bench.

From the kitchen, Mike heard Annie ask, "Are you okay?"

Hugh sighed. "It's…er…spread to my arms and legs. I mean, aches and pains. And I'm baking hot one minute and freezing cold the next."

"I'm worried about you."

"It's nothing."

Mike came out of the kitchen and stood in the doorway. He thought both of them looked unwell.

Seeing Mike, Hugh said, "How are you getting on with the cooker?"

"It's in business." Putting a hand to his forehead, Mike added, "But it burned half my hair away when I got it to light."

"Good stuff." Hugh managed a smile.

"No tin-opener," Annie reported. "I battered my

way into the beans with that fork. It's a multi-purpose tool." She barked a cough and then said, "Lauren can make a raft with it later."

Mike giggled. He knew that Annie was taking a dig at Lauren more than trying to be funny. He returned to the cooker and gave the beans a final stir. Then he called, "Nearly ready. Funny pale colour but no nasty smells."

"Is it one fork between five of us?" Hugh asked.

"No," Mike shouted back. "You can use your fingers."

Hugh looked down at his hands. "They're covered in petrol and gunk."

"You're lucky. Might give your beans a bit of flavour," Mike said, as he joined the others and they went into the living room.

Annie blew her nose. Pulling open one of the drawers under the tabletop, she announced, "Crisis over. There's more cutlery here."

Then, in an instant, her face turned sickly white and she collapsed. Her head crashed against the corner of the table and blood spurted from the wound.

14

Sitting outside, his back propped against the dead tree, Mike turned to look at Annie. He could barely see anything, but she was breathing in the night air as if she'd just come up to the surface after a long underwater dive. A bandage from the first-aid kit had stopped the alarming flow of blood. Her T-shirt was stained around the shoulder and front.

"You look like a footballer after a clash of heads," Mike whispered. "You should've said you were feeling bad."

Annie smiled weakly. "I leave complaining to wimps."

"What wimps?"

"Boys."

Mike nodded. "Everyone knows us boys suffer much more." His grin soon faded. He was still surprised by the emotional jolt he'd felt when he'd seen Annie fall; when he'd seen her blood. He was aware that being with Annie was changing him. He suspected that the island was changing him as well. "Are you going to be all right?" he asked her.

"Yeah. It's probably nothing. A summer cold, stress, lack of food, dodgy baked beans…"

"You went down before you had the beans." Mike knew she was playing down her state of health, but he didn't know if she was doing it for his benefit or her own. "Lauren knows about temperature," he said softly. "She says you've got a fever. What if it's…you know?"

Choking slightly on her words, she said, "The rapid and invariably fatal Agent A?"

Mike couldn't bear to think about the possibility of her dying. It wouldn't be fair. Why pick on Annie? He hated the idea that she could have caught something that hadn't affected him. It made him feel guilty.

Annie let out a powerful sneeze. "If that's what I've got, you shouldn't be this close. I should confine myself to the stables."

Maybe, to stay brave, she needed him to refuse to believe that she could be seriously ill. "No. You're right. You just needed fresh air, or more food. I'll catch some fish for you in the morning."

"Do you know how?"

"I've fished before."

"So, what are you going to use as bait?"

Mike took a deep breath. "Ah. Yes. No sign of worms or anything else round here."

"That's why I suggested mackerel. They'll snap at anything shiny. A spinner or silver paper. So stupid they deserve to be eaten. I'll show you when it gets light."

Mike was amazed that she could be so calm and tough. That was one reason he liked her so much. When it came to courage, he didn't doubt for a second that she could put most boys to shame. Maybe it ran in the Firth family, though, because Hugh was battling on as well.

Mike said, "I know me and Hugh don't exactly see eye to eye all the time, but…"

"What?"

"He's really trying. If I was as sick as him, I'd probably go and lie down somewhere and groan a lot. But he's keeping going – for the rest of us."

Annie nodded. "He likes you, you know."

Mike was surprised. "Really?"

"Yes. He wouldn't admit it, but he likes your spirit of adventure, I think. Wishes he had some of it."

"What about Daniel? He keeps himself to himself."

"Mmm." Annie thought for a moment and then said, "Behind that quiet exterior, plenty's going on. He's very smart, very perceptive. And he's tougher than he looks. If you need someone on your side, you could do a lot worse than Daniel." She paused again before adding, "It's a pity Claudia's not here."

"Your mysterious sister."

"Sometimes I think she beamed down from a different planet. It was strange when Mum and Dad decided to adopt her. They just wanted to help her but it's a bit difficult – she suffers from ADHD."

"You mean that attention-seeking hyperactive thing? So she plays up, flops at school and wants to be in the spotlight all the time – like the rest of us?"

"Taken to extremes. She's…got attitude. She never seems to listen – actually, I think she does but she's too busy flitting from one thing to another. Wherever she goes, she takes things. She's got millions of newspaper clippings all over her room. She cuts things out of books and magazines in the library. Gets into trouble for that."

"Is she too busy doing her own thing to be here with us then?"

Annie glanced at him. "We do try to involve her, Mike. We really do. But she's too scatty. When we're ready to do something with her, she's gone off somewhere else. It doesn't take much to distract her."

"Isn't there a fix?"

"Sort of, but Mum and Dad don't believe in controlling her with drugs. They call it a chemical cosh."

"So why would it be good to have her here?"

Annie smiled. "She's got a knack for fishing. The fish line up to throw themselves on her hook. We wouldn't go hungry if she was here. As long as we could keep her mind on the job long enough. Anyway," she added, "what about *your* sister? She'll be missing you."

"Will she? She'll be pleased to have me out of the way."

"That's just the impression she wants to give you. It won't be how she really feels."

Mike shook his head. "You're guessing. If she misses me, it'll be because she hasn't got anyone to fight with."

"I bet your mum'll be panicking – like my folks."

"No chance," Mike answered. "Maybe if she knew I was in a mess, but usually she's glad to see the back of me."

"Does that mean she's used to you disappearing? Do you stay out overnight quite a lot?"

"It's not the first time," he said. "But…"

"What?"

"Just with mates. Not with a girl." Feeling embarrassed, Mike rested his head on the bark of the tree and looked up. There was a thin slice of moon and the stars were clear against a massive black sky. "There's a lot of open space around here, you know.

Too much for me. I can't get used to how dark it is. I don't think I've ever seen real darkness before."

"What about the campsite?" said Annie.

"It's next to a karaoke club, sports club and noisy pub. Nothing like this."

"You should get out more. At night. Preferably at sea."

"People say it's scary, but it isn't."

Annie laughed quietly. "No. It's lovely. Look at the stars."

"I never knew there were so many."

"There's a satellite up there somewhere as well. It's blocked us out, though. That's the scary bit."

Sensing a change in Annie's mood, Mike twisted round to gaze at her. "Are you scared?"

"Not of the dark. But this island, its history, Agent A... Yes. I'm scared."

Mike had met Annie by chance only days ago. Now, realizing how lucky he'd been, he felt a tingling throughout his body. For the first time in his life, he wanted to be totally open and honest with someone. He would never hide anything from her. "Me too," he admitted.

15

Claudia didn't trust the man and woman sitting opposite her. He had a beard and she was too thin. Claudia jumped up, went to the desk and flicked through the hotel's tourist information, then she turned on the TV.

"No. Not now, love." Dad used the zapper to turn it off again.

She sat down on the carpet in a huff.

What sort of people were they anyway? Police or something? Messing up her day. Messing up her holiday. Why did she have to speak to them? And why was everyone getting excited anyway? If she was the one who'd vanished, no one would be bothered. It'd probably be a relief to them all.

She stabbed the scissors into Dad's newspaper.

It was Ms. Thin who tried next. "Claudia. It's very important that you tell us if you know anything about where your sister and brothers went."

She finished cutting around the photo of some celebrity coming out of a clinic, before going back to the desk and rearranging the tea-making facilities. She picked up Daniel's puzzle book and glanced at a half-completed brainteaser, then dropped it again.

"Did they say anything to you about what they intended to do?"

Claudia stopped and stared at Ms. Thin for a

moment. She shook her head. "They never tell me anything."

"Think, Claudia," her mum said. "Are you sure?"

"I'm hungry. I'm going to have the biscuits."

When Mrs. Firth's mobile rang, she almost leaped out of her chair. She snatched up the phone eagerly and said, "Yes?"

"Is there any news?"

Straight away, she recognized the voice of Lauren's mum. "Oh. Sorry. I thought it might be... Er, no. We've had the police here. The coastguard's going out to search. We've done all we can. There've been no reports of the boat...so far."

"I wish I was up there with you," said Mrs. Douglas. "I feel so helpless just sitting here waiting."

"I'm sure they're all right. They're very responsible. Particularly Hugh – and Lauren."

"I can understand their mobiles being out of

range but why isn't the radio working?" There was a rising sense of panic in Mrs. Douglas's voice.

Mrs. Firth tried to sound calm. "We can only think it's developed a fault. They're probably on their way back right now. I hope so."

"Who's this boy Mike who's with them?"

"I don't know much about him, I'm afraid." When her children had failed to return by nightfall, Mrs. Firth had begun to wonder about him too. But she didn't want to alarm Lauren's mother. "Our Annie took up with him a few days ago, so he'll be fine. She wouldn't go off with just anyone." She paused before adding, "There's one thing, though. I ought to tell his family what's happening, but I don't know how to contact them."

"Well, I don't like my Lauren mixing with boys I don't know. I'm worried in case he's got something to do with this."

"I don't see how he could," Mrs. Firth replied, hoping it was true. "Besides, Hugh and Lauren wouldn't stand for any nonsense." Mrs. Firth was feeling guilty not only because she hadn't checked out Annie's new friend, but also because she hadn't demanded to know exactly where her kids were going. She hadn't done what a mother was supposed to do.

Mrs. Douglas said, "I just hope they're okay."

"I think I'd feel it if anything had happened... you know."

"Let's pray you're right," Lauren's mum replied.

The breeze came in through the door and ballooned the tent. Mike's mum laughed. "He's gone off with a girl – who knows what sort of girl – and before you know it, he's out all night!" Her head and throat were sore after a heavy night in the karaoke club. "Just like his dad. Never does things by half. Never tells me what he's up to."

Normally, when Mike was around, his sister was all tantrums and tears – always up for a scrap with her brother. Now, she was missing him. "When's he coming back?" she asked.

"By the end of the week or we go home without him." Seeing the sudden look of alarm on her daughter's face, she shook her head and smiled. "Not really. But he'd better put in an appearance tomorrow or he's in deep trouble."

16

It was an unhappy sleepover. Still groggy, but feeling pressure on his arm, Daniel stirred. It was Mike, back from his turn on night watch, prodding him. "Has anyone come?" Daniel whispered so that he didn't disturb the others.

Mike shook his head. "It's time for you to take over, that's all."

Daniel looked around the central room. Annie, Hugh and Lauren were lying on horsehair mattresses that were barely softer than the floor, covered with blankets from the survival kits. Daniel scrambled silently to his feet and pushed the button on his watch to illuminate its face. Surprised, he looked at Mike who was settling onto the mattress in his place. Annie's boyfriend had given him an extra two hours of sleep. It was nearly dawn.

"Thank you," he murmured.

A glimmer of daybreak penetrated the wing where animals had once been housed. The faint light was enough for Daniel. He grabbed the heavy fishing rod from the wall and checked that the corroded reel and spinner were still in working order. Then he made for the jetty where they'd landed. The back door to the island, as Lauren had called it. There, he would catch breakfast, even if the fishing gear was well past its best.

Daniel didn't want to cross the circle where

animals had been exposed to Agent A. Instead, he walked round the experimental site and then down towards the water's edge, where fragments of his former life were strewn over the rocks. That was all there was. He couldn't see any ships. Scanning the still brightening sky, he couldn't see any aircraft either. The day was going to be cloudier and breezier than yesterday.

Daniel preferred sitting by the sea to hanging around a bleak cottage. The normal sounds of waves and wind were somehow reassuring on this ghostly island.

He examined the spinner again and, wasting no time, cast it as far as he could with the old clumsy rod. For a few seconds, he allowed the silvery spinner to sink, and then he began to reel it in unevenly. To any passing mackerel, it would look like a tasty wounded fish.

Being on lookout was an opportunity for Daniel to think things through. Big brother Hugh thought

18

Claudia wasn't interested in Ms. Thin and Mr. Beard's aerial photographs of the floating fragments of a boat. She wasn't interested in her dad's identification of the wreckage. She wasn't interested in the official explanation: "The motor cruiser seems to have hit an object to the north of here. There was no sign of... There's still a search but...I'm sorry... There's no land anywhere near. They're now classed as missing, presumed drowned."

She wasn't interested in adult tears. Claudia stopped listening and charged into her own room in the hotel suite.

This has happened before, she told herself. Ages ago. She was certain. Embarking on a search of her box of newspaper stories that she'd collected on their trip, she flung cuttings around like confetti. "It's here somewhere." But where?

Claudia gave up looking for whatever it was that she'd lost and started fiddling with the radio. The reception was lousy. So was the music. And the talk stations were boring.

Instead, she grabbed the map. She opened it out and traced the path across the sea that Daniel and Hugh had shown her. She remembered Hugh's finger. It went south. "Why don't you come? Look. We can explore down here, then across to the mainland and these islands. The coast's supposed to

be great. Maybe we can find a bay for swimming."
She'd agreed. But somehow she'd ended up going
out. She'd missed the boat. She wasn't bothered
about swimming anyway. The only good bit about
swimming was watching her fingertips going
wrinkly, but she could make them do that by taking
a long bath.

Hugh's finger had gone south, though. Not north.
South.

In her mind, she could see his forefinger sliding
over the exact course they'd planned to take.

She pushed the map to one side and there it was.
A piece she'd torn out of a book called *Strange
Scottish Stories* that she'd seen downstairs in the
hotel lounge. It had been written last year by a local
reporter called Sheila Welsh. It was based on Mrs.
Betty MacLeod's recollections of a shipwreck from
sixty years ago, just after she'd got married to one of
the three who were declared drowned. Two men and
a woman. The location and bodies had never been

found but the authorities had told Betty that wreckage had been seen a long way from where she thought her husband had gone. The weather had been totally calm, so it wasn't a storm that did for them. According to Sheila Welsh, it was a complete mystery.

Claudia wasn't interested in Betty MacLeod. She looked at least four hundred years old in the photo in the book.

Claudia went back into the main room of the family suite like a whirlwind. "Mum. Dad. I'm going out. Don't wait up."

"What? How can you...? Not at a time like this!"

"Especially at a time like this." She ignored their shocked tearful faces and flew out of the door before she heard more objections or they asked her to explain.

She couldn't explain. She didn't have a clue what she was doing. Or why. They were presumed drowned. What could she do? They weren't even her real sister and brothers. In a DNA test, they'd clump together and she'd be the odd one out. So, why should she care? But she knew Thin and Beard were lying. And "presumed" didn't mean definitely. She had to go south. She had to check it out for herself.

It would be difficult to handle the motorized yacht on her own but she thought she could do it. She'd seen her parents do it enough times. She could do anything if she put her mind to it.

19

Mike began to fear the worst. He began to think that Daniel was right. When Annie had last hauled herself to the toilet, she'd told him she'd seen blood. Her body seemed to be leaking the stuff. And her skin had become an exaggerated pink in places. Lauren thought it meant that she was bleeding inside.

What could Mike – or the others – do about it? He couldn't pick up a phone and call for help. He couldn't make a doctor appear by magic, or by parachute. He couldn't stagger with her to the nearest surgery or hospital. He could pray for help, but he was fairly sure that no one would be listening. He hadn't got the faintest idea how to build a raft. Even if he had, he wouldn't know how to steer it or in which direction. He felt helpless.

A few metres away, Hugh was also drooping on a mattress and groaning. He complained that he was cold all over, except for his lungs, which were on fire. His throat and chest were so tight that the simple act of breathing in and out seemed to use all of his energy.

The rest of them tried to keep busy. They tried to be useful. Daniel had just returned from keeping watch and fishing. Lauren had taken on the role of nurse. Mike was chef and odd-job man. As cook, he didn't need a wide range of skills. He just had to gut mackerel and put them under the grill. He'd seen his grandma preparing fish and he just copied what she did. It wasn't pretty. The slippery innards spewing out of the punctured fish turned his stomach, but it had to be done. Annie and Hugh were well beyond eating, but he had to keep himself and the others alive.

Even Annie had a job. She was trying to read Jack's notebook from cover to cover. She wasn't managing very well because she was so feeble. Her eyes drifted in and out of focus and she drifted in and out of sleep. She would read a page and then, apparently not having taken in a single word, she would read it again. She would lose concentration halfway through. Sometimes, she looked bemused. Her brain didn't seem capable of understanding what she had read.

Her obvious frustration with her meandering mind and useless body seemed to be reaching a peak when suddenly she found something that grabbed her attention. "I think you ought to hear this," she said. "It's right at the end of the notebook. I didn't see it before. It's…er… Well, listen. You decide." In her croaky voice, she read out the final notes: "*Conventional anthrax does not transfer easily from an infected person to a healthy one. Individuals who are in close proximity tend to become ill because they touch the same contaminated source or breathe the same contaminated air. However, the new strain created for our final experiments is unusually contagious. Initial results show that Agent Ac, as we have named it, can be transmitted directly from one infected animal to a test subject. We had already put ourselves at risk of infection before we became aware of this property.*"

Mike interrupted. "Is this English?"

The others hushed him.

"*There is no known cure for the disease, but we have urgently requested specialized treatment at the best possible medical establishment. We are about to evacuate the island but, given that human-to-human transfer is very likely, I expect that we will not be welcome on the mainland. I write this note in case events transpire against us. I fear that my return to Betty may be delayed indefinitely."*

No one reacted straight away.

Then Lauren said, "So that's it. Daniel was right. They got rid of the scientists to stop them spreading the disease and now they're leaving us here to rot as well!"

"*Won't be welcome on the mainland,*" Hugh sighed. "That's an understatement. It's a fair bet the Government blasted them out of the water."

Daniel nodded. "In a way, their experiments were too successful."

"What are we going to do?" asked Lauren.

"Let's get this straight," said Mike. "If we stay here, we die. If we escape, we poison everyone else. Is that right?"

"Not easy, is it?" Annie replied.

Daniel surprised them all. "You're wrong. It's dead easy. We try as hard as we can to get away. We've got to. If we warn them we've got this disease, they can put us in an isolation ward. Then we won't hurt anyone else. Like Jack said, they should give us the best hospital. They owe us that, even if they can't do anything for us."

Mike was surprised for a different reason. Daniel had not stammered. Not once.

"They don't owe us anything," Lauren cried. "We shouldn't have come here. It's our fault."

"They should have built a big wall round it," said Mike.

"There was a warning sign," Lauren reminded him. "You ignored it."

"That's not helping," Hugh said quietly.

Lauren glanced down at her boyfriend. "We've still got to get away."

Mike shook his head. "I've got mates. And a sister. What if I gave her this…?"

Lauren butted in. "You're not sick, are you? Perhaps you, me and Daniel are in the clear."

Mike hesitated. "What are you saying? We've got to escape and leave Annie and Hugh here because they're in a bad way? No chance!"

"Just because we're not feeling sick doesn't mean we haven't got it," Daniel said. "We might just be lagging behind. Maybe it'll be our turn tomorrow."

Annie struggled to add, "Even if you're okay, I think you could be carrying the disease – on your clothes or whatever."

"If we'd taken a vote on landing here," Lauren said, "we'd have sailed away. We wouldn't be in this mess."

"So what?" Mike asked.

"We could take a vote now," Lauren suggested, "on whether we stay or work out how to get away. I vote we go."

"It doesn't matter much," Mike said, "because we can't go anywhere."

"It's about what we *try* to do," Lauren snapped.

"We mustn't spread it to everyone else," said Annie. "We've got to isolate ourselves."

Mike agreed with his girlfriend at once. "Good call."

Lauren sighed. "Two votes to one. Daniel?"

"I've already said. It's not a choice of staying here or going and infecting everyone else. We try and get away to a hospital. Then it's their job to stop the germ spreading."

Lauren nodded. "Two all." She looked directly at Hugh. "It's all down to you."

20

While they waited for Hugh's decision, Mike watched Lauren wiping the goo from around her boyfriend's mouth. Mike felt that her heart wasn't in it. She was going through the motions like a trained nurse who cared but didn't get emotionally involved. Her arm was outstretched as if she didn't want to get too close. Maybe she was scared.

Until he'd come to this island, Mike had never thought about dying. Why should he? It was too distant to worry about. He knew that no one lived for ever, but medicine could fix almost every illness. He'd assumed that doctors would have learned to fix the rest by the time he was old enough to catch any of them. He'd expected a long life and a lot of fun. He wanted the same for the others. But the island had thrown it all into doubt. They were teenagers – far too young to go down with something incurable and fatal. It wasn't right.

Mike had been knocked sideways by Annie's sickness. He was sitting beside her, his hand on her arm. Hugh would have called him reckless to stay so close to an infected person. He would think that Lauren was being much more sensible. After all, he wouldn't want to pass the disease on to his girlfriend. That would be Hugh's dilemma. He could be comforted by her presence or he could avoid infecting her by keeping his distance. He couldn't do both.

Hugh opened his bloodshot eyes. He gazed at Lauren and then at Annie. Mike wasn't sure who he was speaking to when he said, "I wish I'd tried harder with Claudia."

"We could've been more patient with her," Annie replied in a whisper.

"We could've tried to understand her problems instead of counting her as one of ours."

Annie agreed. "She probably wasn't as annoying as we made out."

Hugh moved his head. It was supposed to be a nod. "Talking of annoying people..." He glanced towards Mike.

Annie smiled. "Yeah but he's cute."

Mike gulped. "Cute? Me? I'd rather be annoying."

For a moment, Hugh's eyes sparkled. "Definitely more annoying than cute." Shifting his gaze to Annie, Hugh continued as if Mike wasn't listening. "But he's okay because he really cares about you."

"I know," Annie replied softly.

"How are you feeling?" Hugh asked his sister.

"Like I'm going through a spin cycle."

"Yes. You look like it." Hugh turned his head. Talking to Lauren, he added, "I think it's time you built your raft. It won't have to hold five after all. You've got my vote, Lauren. Go, before you catch this thing from me or Annie."

21

The Head of the Security Service stood up and paced anxiously around the room. "I'm looking for a way out of this situation," she said to her MI5 advisor. "An *acceptable* way out."

"We are speaking off the record, aren't we?"

"Yes."

"Well, in that case, it's not straightforward. These

children aren't simply contaminated with anthrax. If that had been the case, we could isolate them, burn their clothing and put them through an antibiotic scrub to decontaminate them. But it's not like that. This is Agent Ac. As soon as they clambered onto the island, they were going to catch the disease. Some quicker than others. They'll be infectious. You can decontaminate people's outsides but not their insides. By now, the blood, lungs and other organs of the first casualties will be heaving with anthrax. It's way beyond what an ordinary hospital can handle. If they were to come back to the mainland, they'd pass it on sooner or later by coughing, sneezing, kissing or touching. Actually, just breathing and talking will do it. In the circumstances, sacrificing five is a good deal."

"Are we sure they're still alive?"

"The motion detector keeps pinging. At least one's still moving. We don't know enough about the agent or the children to predict how quickly they'll fall victim to it. In forty-seven, the Government decided it was too dangerous to continue the research."

"Mmm. What about sending a military doctor to the island in full protective gear?"

"For what purpose?" the advisor asked.

"To try and cure them with modern medicine."

"Vaccination would only work before exposure to the agent. It's too late for that. Large doses of some modern antibiotics might prevent death but only if they're administered very quickly after infection. The RAF pilot was convinced they'd already walked across the most contaminated area – the bomb site. Some – maybe all – of them will have contracted the disease right there. Once it takes hold, it produces poisons in sufficient quantities to kill even if they're given an antibiotic. Agent Ac is a very effective biological weapon. Virtually untreatable once it's in among people."

The security chief completed a circuit of her office in silence. Then she came to a decision. She said,

"If they're at the untreatable stage, there's no point treating them on the island or anywhere else. If some of them aren't showing symptoms yet, we might have the drugs to save them—"

The advisor interrupted. "That's a long shot at best."

"But it's possible, even though there's a huge risk in going down that road."

"Yes."

"As I said," the security chief continued, "I'm looking for an acceptable way out. It strikes me this is more about politics than medicine. If we rescued the treatable ones, they'd talk to the press, the full story would emerge and we'd have more explaining to do than is politically acceptable. We'd have to explain why we pronounced five innocent youngsters dead when they were still alive, and why we quarantined them on the island by destroying their boat." She put up her hand to stop her advisor interrupting again. "Yes, I know. I can justify it. It's what MI5's for. I'm charged with the duty of keeping the population safe and what we did was to protect the nation. But giving five kids a death sentence on a non-existent island wouldn't play well with the press or the public."

The advisor's job was to provide guidance, not to be influenced by emotion. In a calm and measured voice, he replied, "We mustn't forget the most important factor, which is that there are extreme health implications if you decide to attempt any sort of rescue."

"Yes. It grieves me enormously but, for the good of everyone else, we're going to let nature take its course."

"And what about the remaining sister? Claudia Firth."

The Head of MI5 came to an abrupt halt. "What about her?"

"She's gone missing, I understand, along with the family yacht."

"Does she know where the others went?"

"She says not but…" The advisor shrugged.

"Find her. If she knows – if she goes anywhere near the island – take every step to stop her. She *cannot* be allowed to rescue them if they're still alive. She'd put every one of us in danger. We can't let that happen."

22

Mike looked at the five planks of wood pulled from the paddock and swore. "Maybe if we had screws and a drill..."

"But we don't," Lauren said. "We've got wood and rope. That's all."

Mike sighed. "There was a needle and thread in the cottage."

"When are you going to take this seriously?" Lauren retorted.

"I am," Mike replied. "I've just seen Annie coughing blood. I'm taking it very seriously. I was just…" The words wouldn't come.

Daniel helped him out. "You were just saying it's a tough job – in your own way."

"Yes. But I don't think we're doing the right thing anyway, remember. We could kill a lot of people."

"Well, I don't want to die here," Lauren said. "This is our only hope."

"You're being…you know."

"What?"

"Selfish, I suppose."

"I d-don't think so," Daniel replied. "If you'd got really bad flu, you'd expect a hospital to look after you without passing it round everyone else."

"That's right," Lauren agreed. "Now let's concentrate on what we're doing."

Mike did not feel like concentrating. "Even if we

make something that floats, how are we going to get Annie and Hugh on it?"

Lauren was about to answer but then changed her mind. "Let's just make it and worry about that afterwards."

Mike stared at her. "You don't want to take them, do you? You want to leave them behind!"

"That's not true! It's just that…"

"What?"

Flustered, Lauren blurted out, "You were there when Hugh said it, weren't you? 'It won't have to hold five.' That's him talking, not me. Anyway, it'd be easier for three of us to get away, wouldn't it? Then we can send a doctor back for them."

"I'm not going without Annie," Mike stated flatly.

"There's no point arguing till we've got ourselves a boat, is there? If we can't build something, none of us are leaving."

"Did you mean it?" Mike asked. "You'd make

sure a doctor came back for Annie and Hugh?"

"Sure."

Mike took a deep breath and then threw up his arms. "Okay. But I don't think we're going to make a raft like this. What about the dead tree outside the cottage? If we could chop it down, you could ride out on it, with the planks as sort of stabilizers."

"A bit like a catamaran," Daniel said.

"I guess so."

"Have you seen an axe?" Lauren said impatiently. "Or a big saw?"

Mike shook his head. "That's the problem."

"Not the only problem. There's only three of us to drag it to the sea."

"And I still don't know how we'd attach the stabilizers with rope…"

Daniel interrupted. "We've got to set fire to this stuff right now."

"What? Why?"

"Because it'd get the attention of that yacht."

"Yacht?" Mike looked around madly, his heart thumping.

Lauren put a hand on her brow. "Yes! Way over there." She was virtually jumping up and down with excitement. Then, suddenly, she stopped and gazed intently at the boat. "Isn't it...?" She looked at Daniel.

Daniel nodded. "I think so."

"What are you two talking about?" Mike shouted in frustration.

Lauren answered, "It's Daniel's mum and dad!"

"It's our yacht," Daniel said. "I'd recognize the profile anywhere, but I d-don't know about Mum and D-Dad."

"How do you mean? Who else would it be?"

"Mum and D-Dad d-didn't know where we went. Hugh showed Claudia more or less where we were going on a map. I bet it's Claudia."

"Maybe it's all of them," Lauren said. "I don't care who it is as long as they see us."

Mike thought for a moment. "You *should* care. Whoever it is, they're going to get infected."

Lauren wasn't listening. "They're sailing right past, aren't they?" she said in panic. "They're not coming this way."

The boys watched for a few seconds – until it was obvious that Lauren was right.

"They can't just go past and leave us!"

Daniel yelled, "I'll get some paraffin and the matches." He sprinted towards the cottage.

Behind him, Lauren began stacking together anything that would burn.

23

The GPS system told Claudia that there was no land to starboard so she didn't pay any attention to the small deceptive lump on the horizon. It was an optical illusion. She liked puzzles that were based on optical illusions. Back home, she had a great picture of blue dots on a yellow background. When she looked at it, the image seemed to ripple like the sea. Really weird. Things were not always what they appeared to be. She maintained her course to the south.

But what was she doing? What was she looking for? She was hardly likely to see any bodies or wreckage floating in the vast expanse of ocean. So, what was the point of this wild goose chase? If their cruiser had hit something, the tide would have dispersed the wreckage. If they had overturned, the boat would have sunk. Either way, the bodies would have floated away or gone under. They might even have been eaten.

Everyone in the family liked eating fish, apart from her. Salmon was the worst. Yuck. Horrible colour as well. Maybe fish had got their own back on Hugh, Annie and Daniel.

Perhaps they'd veered towards the mainland and the offshore islands. Hugh said it was supposed to be great there. Maybe that's where they'd gone – to find a bay for swimming. They liked to swim. She wasn't bothered. Maybe they'd got into trouble trying to steer into an inlet and hit rock.

Somewhere overhead – above the clouds – an aeroplane roared briefly before the noise of its engines dwindled to nothing. Distracted, Claudia looked around. And she saw something. Something very odd. Something that couldn't possibly happen. She saw smoke coming out of the sea.

That optical illusion – the bump on the horizon – was too far away to see now, but smoke was coming from the same direction.

Was it a peculiar type of cloud that she'd never seen before? Or was it some sort of signal? It was definitely a mystery worth investigating. She took hold of the wheel and spun it round.

A few minutes later, she could see the bump again. Not an optical illusion after all. It was definitely rock emerging from the sea, and there were flames. That meant there were probably people who'd lit a fire. Unless it was spontaneous combustion. Some dead people caught fire for no reason and smouldered away for days until just their hands and feet were left. Everything else was black ash. Fantastic. Anyway, what she was seeing wasn't bodies on fire. Too much smoke for that. Besides, it wasn't hot today. Spontaneous combustion of something outside needed lots of sunshine, she imagined.

Looking ahead as she made for the island that wasn't on the chart, she noticed it didn't have any trees. It couldn't be a wood on fire. So, there must be people with matches and a reason to light a bonfire.

She liked fireworks. Ones that whizzed round and round were her favourite. But they wouldn't be any good in daytime like this. It wasn't even November.

Closer to the island, she could just make out three people on the coast. They were waving their arms like mad.

She also saw a helicopter heading for the same spot. Claudia liked helicopters. She'd had a flight in one once. It was at Land's End and it swerved around the cliffs. Someone behind her had brought up bucketloads of sick but she'd thought the trip was brilliant. Hanging on to the yacht's wheel with one hand, she jumped up and down and waved the other at the approaching aircraft.

24

Daniel, Lauren and Mike had left the smoking fire and gone down to the jetty.

"She's seen us!" Daniel cried. "She's coming this way. Look. I told you it'd be Claudia." Planning ahead, he added, "She won't be able to get in close. It's too shallow for the yacht. Can you two swim?"

"Yes," Lauren replied excitedly.

Mike sounded anything but excited. "Annie and Hugh can't. Not in their state."

"We're going to go and get help," Daniel reminded him.

"All right," Mike agreed, "but I'm staying with them till it arrives. They might need me."

It was then that they heard the sound they most dreaded, bringing their optimism to an abrupt end – the thrashing of rotor blades.

On the yacht, Claudia was bouncing around and waving like a child who had never seen a chopper before.

"What on earth is she doing?" Lauren shouted. "She's crazy."

Daniel shook his head. "She d-doesn't know what it means."

"He'll open fire," Mike said.

"Yes." Then Daniel realized what he had to do. "Catch this!" he said, throwing his precious mobile phone to Lauren. It might have no reception, but the battery was still charged. "Stay here and film what happens."

Daniel was about to make a dash to the edge of the rock and dive in when Mike grabbed his arm and held him back.

"You could pass the disease on to her!"

Daniel hesitated but only for a moment. "I've got to risk it or she'll get blown up."

Nodding, Mike let go of his arm.

The cold water hit Daniel like a body punch, but he ignored the shock. Using front crawl – his fastest stroke – he made for the yacht. When he got close, he stopped swimming and looked up. Claudia had cut the engine. She was standing by the ladder, looking puzzled. But, in an instant, she forgot about Daniel and turned towards the helicopter that was about to circle the boat. Daniel put on a burst of speed, grasped the struts of the ladder and clambered up.

"Get ready to jump," he yelled at Claudia.

He ran to the stern, opened the safety box and

grabbed the inflatable life raft. Hoping that the pilot could not see what he was doing, he tied its rope hurriedly round his waist.

"We're going overboard!" he cried.

"What?"

"He's going to blow us up. Jump! Dive down and stay down as long as you can."

It was incredibly dangerous. The weight of the life raft, wrapped up like a birthday present, would act like an anchor and drag Daniel down. He just had to hope that the water wasn't too deep. If he had to undo the knot so that he didn't drown, the inflatable would be lost at the bottom of the sea.

"Ready?"

"You're supposed to be dead," said Claudia.

"Jump or both of us will be." With the inflatable in one hand, Daniel grabbed Claudia's arm with the other and leaped with her from the back of the yacht.

Immediately, the weight around his waist yanked him down and ripped Claudia's arm out of his grasp.

He had to hope that, like last time, the RAF had no interest in killing them. He had to hope that the idea was simply to disable the yacht. And he had to hope that the helicopter pilot hadn't seen what Daniel had taken overboard with him.

There was a booming thud in his ears and suddenly the water around him seemed to boil. He was buffeted helplessly and he tumbled away from the blast. Fragments of fibreglass, metal and plastic shot past him. His last breath of air burst from his lungs in a mass of bubbles but still he refused to surface.

He wasn't sinking any further. The emergency raft must have lodged itself on the bottom. He untied the rope from around his waist and clutched the end tightly in his right hand. Knowing that he was going to run out of air any second, he made for the surface. It wasn't easy to lift the dead weight of the inflatable, but he kicked as powerfully as he could and made his way up slowly, painfully slowly, towards the light. It felt like swimming through treacle but, within seconds, he burst through the surface and gulped the air.

Coughing and spluttering, he looked round. The helicopter was heading off. What remained of the yacht was sinking. "Claudia? Where are you? Are you all right?"

Behind him, she cried out, "Wow! That was great."

Daniel didn't want to inflate the life raft. Not when there was a chance that the pilot might look back and see it. "Help me with this." He showed her the rope. "We've got to drag it to the shore."

The yacht's escape pod had its own waterproof battery. As soon as Daniel hit the button, the capsule unfolded itself on the shore like some giant toy. The pump kicked in and it inflated before their eyes. It was circular, a bit like a paddling pool. There was nothing in it but a few flares, a flare gun and an emergency transmitter. Daniel didn't turn the transmitter on. He didn't want to broadcast an SOS signal until they were well away from the island. And until the RAF helicopter had long since gone.

Mike looked down at the life raft. "How do you drive it?"

"We d-don't," Daniel answered. "We d-drift in it. But at least we get away. And once we're well away, I'll switch the emergency beacon on. Any shipping will pick up the signal and come to rescue us."

Lauren nodded. "Let's get it in the water. The sooner we get away—"

"Hang on," Daniel said. "Everything's changed now. Using this instead of the yacht, we d-don't have to swim out. We can all get in. Including Hugh and Annie. It's d-designed to take up to eight. All right, Mike? We'll have to go back to the cottage to help them, but the four of us can d-do it."

Lauren looked hurt. "I was going to say, the sooner we get away, the sooner we can get help."

"It's easier for us all to go and then tell the port authorities before we get too close that we need to be isolated," said Daniel. "That way, no one's got to risk coming back here and we don't hurt anyone else."

Mike agreed with Daniel. "Okay. Let's go and get them. Me and Claudia can lift Annie. You and Lauren can manage Hugh."

Claudia looked bewildered. "What's wrong with them? What cottage? Thin and Beard said you were all dead. What's going on?"

"It's a long story. We'll tell you as we go. And you can tell us how we d-died." Daniel paused before adding, "I'm sorry we need you to help, Claudia."

"Why sorry?" she asked.

"Because you could catch the d-disease. You could get it from Annie, the island, or any of us when we're in the life raft together. That's the mess we've got you into."

25

The life raft felt flimsy. It rocked and rolled with the waves as if it were about to flood with water and sink, but it didn't. They were sitting in a circle, backs against the inflated wall, feet tangling in the middle. Blood was seeping from Annie onto the flexible plastic base. No one mentioned it to her or asked where it was coming from.

"Look," said Mike, pointing across the waves.

"What?"

"You can't see the island any more."

Lauren was subdued. "Isn't it time we switched this SOS thing on so boats know we're here?"

Daniel shook his head. "Let's make sure by giving it another half-hour."

"It's been an hour already. We've drifted a long way."

"We need to be out of the area where they block signals."

"How far's that?"

Daniel shrugged and held up his mobile phone. "Still nothing on this."

"That's because we're so far from the nearest radio mast," Lauren said.

"Let's leave it a bit longer before we broadcast where we are. The RAF thinks we're still marooned on the island. If we d-do it now, I'm worried they'll realize it's us and that we've got away somehow.

The further away we are, the less likely they'll work it out and come for us."

"Makes sense to me," Mike said. "And Daniel…"

"What?"

"What you did back there…going onto the yacht when you knew it was going to get hit. That was brave."

Daniel shrugged again. "I couldn't see any other way. But…"

"What?" asked Mike.

"I think what Claudia d-did was tremendous. Let's face it. We weren't going to build a usable raft. We'd still be stuck without her."

Lauren ran her fingertips through her hair as if what she needed most in the whole world was a brush and a mirror. "Let's just hope someone spots us before we get to Greenland or wherever."

Claudia smiled. "Most of Greenland's covered in ice. It's the world's biggest island."

Apparently annoyed by the distraction, Lauren

retorted, "Come off it! What about Australia?"

"That's a continent, not an island."

Daniel laughed to himself. If he could come to terms with his own stammer, he could come to terms with Claudia's awkward and wonderful diversions. But his warm feeling did not last.

He realized that Claudia was bored. He watched her searching Annie's pockets. She extracted Jack's notebook and Annie's mobile. Claudia's own phone was at the bottom of the sea. Putting the notebook down, she sat back again and fiddled with the phone. Like everyone else, she didn't get a signal. Instead, she flicked through the pages of the notebook, but that didn't entertain her for long. She leaned over the side of the life raft and beat the water with both hands.

Annie was unaware of it all.

Daniel didn't say anything out loud, but he was dreadfully sad for Claudia. Because she cared about them, because she'd come looking, she'd probably been contaminated. He might even have infected her himself – when he'd touched her arm on board the yacht. If not then, she would have been exposed to Agent Ac on the island or in this raft. Now she was like everyone else. She wasn't the odd one out any more. If she hadn't bothered about them – if she'd never set out – she would be perfectly safe and well.

When he felt that the time was right, Daniel flicked the switch on the beacon and its LED display began to flash weakly in the daylight, telling them that it was working. At once, the tension in the life raft went up several notches. They were now more on edge than ever. Their anticipation of rescue was spiced with fear. Lauren wasn't alone in looking nervously up at the sky every few seconds. Who would answer their silent call for help? A cargo ship, a passenger ferry, a tourist's boat, or a helicopter? They were a very easy target and this time they had no safety net. Then there was the matter of disease. Daniel believed they were all going to die from anthrax poisoning. He didn't want them to infect anyone else, but he was desperate to get back to the mainland. Dead or alive, his plan to reveal the truth would fail if he remained at sea.

First it was just a rapidly moving smudge on the horizon. Then it became a motor boat, prow out of the waves, pounding the water, creating sea spray. As it neared, Daniel could see that it was a patrol boat called *Janitor* and it had a single passenger.

"Is this good or bad?" Lauren muttered.

"Not sure," he replied.

"It's fast," Claudia said enthusiastically.

Even Annie and Hugh had opened their eyes to look at the launch that was about to save or sink them. Neither of them seemed able to move, though.

Janitor's prow fell back into the ocean as the skipper let up on the throttle. He was a chunky man of about thirty in casual waterproof clothing. No sign of a uniform. He looked friendly enough to Daniel. His engine idled as he came within hailing distance but no closer. "What's your problem?" he shouted over the waves.

Claudia put her hands around her mouth and replied, "My boat exploded."

"How many of you are there?"

"Six," Mike yelled back.

"I can only see four."

Mike waved at Annie and Hugh. "They're lying down."

"Hurry up!" Lauren cried impatiently. "Help us."

Janitor's skipper ignored her. "What's wrong with them?"

"Seasick," Daniel answered.

"Are you sure?"

Daniel guessed that the man was worried in case they were entering the country illegally or harbouring a disease. "We're on holiday. Our parents are in Oban," he shouted. "Give us a tow, please. You d-don't have to come close. Just in case." He'd never intended to put anyone in danger by moving within reach.

The skipper disappeared under the launch's canopy for a few minutes.

Lauren was becoming increasingly irritable. "What's he doing?" she barked.

"D-don't know." But Daniel had his suspicions. The boat was bound to have a working radio. He wondered if the skipper was consulting a superior – or maybe the port authority.

When he reappeared, he was holding some sort of harpoon and he was aiming it at them: he'd been sent to stop them.

Talking to herself, Lauren said, "Right. That's it! I've had enough." Then she shouted, "Whatever you're thinking of doing, don't."

He hesitated. "What do you mean?"

Bluffing expertly, Lauren waved her mobile phone at him. "I got a signal. I've called my mum. I've told her exactly what's happening. She knows everything."

The skipper lowered his weapon and went straight back under the canopy.

"Brilliant," Daniel whispered to Lauren. "But he's probably checking on any transmissions around here. He'll find out there haven't been any."

Lauren sank down angrily until she was out of sight. Annie and Hugh were too ill to understand what was going on. Daniel didn't think her bluff would work. It was obvious now that this man was part of the cover-up. He'd be under orders to remove the threat of Agent Ac ever reaching the mainland. And he had a very easy way of ensuring that it got no further.

The skipper came out from under the canopy menacingly, still carrying the harpoon. "Sorry," he yelled, "but this is as far as we can let you go."

Whatever had been holding Lauren together finally snapped. Her head appeared above the wall of the life raft and she shrieked, "Look! I'm fed up and hungry. I'm tired and filthy. I need a shower and new clothes. I've got a headache, my throat's raw and my legs feel like tree trunks. I want to go home! Right? Do you understand?"

"I have my orders." He took aim again.

26

The man on the patrol boat did not have to be particularly accurate. He didn't have to hit anyone. A dart in any part of their escape pod would be enough. Then he would turn back and leave them to their fate. He would have done his duty to the British public.

Daniel held his breath.

A movement next to Daniel caught his eye. Lauren lifted the flare gun onto the side of the inflatable, steadied it with both hands and lined up her shot. Daniel gasped at her audacity. Her trick with the mobile had bought her the time she needed to load the gun. But she'd only have one chance and she'd have to be perfectly precise. He held his breath again as she pulled the trigger. The small blaze of flame accelerated away from her and headed directly for the skipper.

For an instant, Daniel saw open-mouthed horror on the man's face as he dropped his weapon in shock. A split-second later, the flare slammed into his chest and sent him crashing onto the deck.

"Yes!" Lauren cried triumphantly.

Daniel and Mike were open-mouthed as well. Lauren had stunned them into silence. Claudia was waving her arms and cheering.

"Come on!" Lauren shouted. "Do I have to do everything myself? Who's going to volunteer to swim over there before he comes round? Daniel – that's your job, isn't it?"

Fifteen minutes later, they had secured the skipper with rope at the stern and hauled Hugh and Annie from the life raft, like wounded soldiers from a battlefield. Now, they were slumped together on the bench and *Janitor* was powering north-east, making for Oban. Lauren and Claudia were clinging to the starboard rail side by side, letting the spray from the sea give them a cold shower. Refreshed, they went under the canopy where Daniel had taken the wheel. Mike was lookout.

"It's all plain sailing from here," Lauren said cheerfully. "We're as good as home."

"Are we?" Daniel replied.

"Why? What have you seen?" Lauren looked up, fearing that a helicopter was bearing down on them.

"I d-don't mean that. We're still in big trouble. We're carrying a d-disease. They won't let us land."

"How are they going to stop us?"

"I d-don't know. But we'll find out sooner or later. Then we ask to be quarantined."

"Have you radioed anybody? Like the coastguard?"

"You've got to be joking. The coastguard will be in on the d-deal. Call them and they'll give our position to the helicopter. You d-don't want that. It's not a good idea to radio anyone." Daniel jerked a thumb towards the skipper. "The people he was talking to will be monitoring communications. Keep radio silence and they won't know what we're d-doing. As soon as we try to communicate, they'll block it and be on to us like a shot."

"Still no mobile signal," Mike added. "And my battery's low."

Lauren shook her head in annoyance. "They wouldn't dare do anything to us if we could tell someone we're still alive – and what's been going on. They'd have too much explaining to do afterwards, wouldn't they?" She checked her mobile for the hundredth time.

Claudia sat down and played with Annie's phone.

"You're fooling yourself if you think that's our only problem," said Daniel.

"How do you mean?"

"Look at Hugh and Annie! That's all of us in a few d-days. And everyone back home if we pass it on."

Becoming agitated again, Lauren denied it. "No! That's not me. It can't be. There's no way it can happen to me."

"You were great back there, Lauren. But you can't shoot anthrax d-down."

Mike turned towards Daniel. "So, what do we do?"

"Hope we can get a mobile working and contact Mum and D-Dad or whoever – like Lauren says. Then tell them we want to be put in an isolation ward."

"That's right," Lauren said. "A hospital can fix us.

Just because they couldn't cure this thing in the 1940s doesn't mean they can't now, does it? A poxy little germ from ages ago. It's not going to beat me. No way."

Daniel didn't reply. After her heroics, he didn't want to dent her confidence. But he wondered why the authorities were prepared to leave them to die if Agent Ac would surrender so easily to modern medicine.

Lauren pointed ahead. "Look!"

"Yes!" Mike squatted beside Annie and said into her ear, "We can see land, Annie. Hang on a bit longer."

Daniel checked the electronic sea chart. "It's the southern tip of Mull."

"And I've got a mobile signal!" Mike almost shouted. "Weak, but it's there."

"Mine too," said Lauren.

"Try phoning someone," Daniel replied. "Anyone. Tell them we're alive."

"Nothing's happening," Mike said. "I press *Call* and nothing happens."

"Text, then."

"I've already tried," Lauren said. "Nothing. No sign it's gone. Give me your number, Mike. I'll text you."

"Why? I'm right here."

Lauren made a tutting noise like a frustrated teacher. "To test the phone, of course." Once she'd entered his number, she sent him a trial message. Then she looked at him and asked, "Has anything come through?"

"No."

Lauren let out a groan. "I don't believe it! Someone's blocking our calls, aren't they?"

"It's happening." Daniel pointed to the north and reduced engine speed.

"What do you...?" The question died on Mike's lips as he looked towards Mull.

Four dull grey ships were heading menacingly towards them.

"That's some welcoming party." Daniel shuddered, knowing full well there would be no party. He remembered Jack MacLeod's words from his journal of sixty years earlier: *we will not be welcome on the mainland.*

Head down, Claudia ignored it all. Fiddling with Annie's phone, she was lost in her own world.

"Rev up," Mike suggested. "Make a run for it!"

"We can't outpace them," Daniel said. "Anyway, they'll have us on radar."

They stared ahead in gloomy silence. Daniel maintained course towards Oban but he had slowed to a crawl. Within minutes, it became obvious that the vessels were military. The huge guns mounted on the prow of each ship proved that. And they formed a daunting barricade between *Janitor* and the mainland.

Daniel swallowed. If he tried to communicate with the serious firepower in front of him, they would probably blast him to pieces before he could ask for quarantine. His voice quaked when he asked, "Ideas anybody?"

Lauren had used up her quota. It seemed that the others had as well, because no one answered.

Mike was screwing up his face in horror. "We're not going to make it, are we? This is where our luck runs out. We can't beat the whole navy."

"What do we do?" Lauren muttered.

Mike threw his mobile down in anger and frustration. "My battery's dead. Hey, what about yours, Daniel?"

Daniel steered with one hand and checked his phone with the other. Then he shook his head. "Same as before. It's showing a signal but I can't place a call. They're jamming it."

The ships were looking bigger and bigger as they got closer. They also looked more and more frightening. They could crush *Janitor* and hardly notice the collision.

Making them jump, the radio's speaker burst into crackly life. A male voice said, "Calling patrol boat twenty-seven. Come in, *Janitor*."

Daniel looked at Lauren and Mike. "D-do we answer?" he asked.

They both shrugged.

"Maybe they're trying to figure out if it's us or him." Daniel nodded towards the man tied to the rail at the stern.

"Yeah," Lauren agreed. "Perhaps he should've radioed in and he hasn't. They don't know what's going on."

Daniel said, "If we answer..."

Lauren interrupted. "They'll figure it's us and blast us out of the water before we can explain."

Daniel nodded in agreement.

"Patrol boat twenty-seven. Come in, please, *Janitor*."

"If we d-don't answer, they'll know something's wrong anyway."

Glancing towards their prisoner, Mike said, "We could get him to answer. Tell him not to—"

Daniel interrupted. "No way. We couldn't stop him saying whatever he wants. I bet he thinks he's got anthrax by now. He won't care what he says."

Lauren shook her head. "We could threaten to put him with Hugh and Annie to make sure he catches it – unless he tells the navy he sank us."

"That's really nasty," Mike objected.

"It's only a threat. I wouldn't really… Anyway, he tells them he's done the business and he's going through to Oban."

"But they'll see us!"

"*Janitor*. Come in immediately."

Lauren looked around. "We'll have to hide somewhere."

"Where? And how will we know what he's d-doing while we're hiding? He could turn round and make for the island again, or take us to one of the ships."

"But he might not if we threaten him enough," Lauren snapped. "Anyway, you haven't got a better idea."

Claudia stood up and said, "I have." Before they could stop her, she snatched the microphone and answered the call. "Hello?"

"Identify yourself," the voice replied bluntly.

The others shook their heads frantically. "Don't!" Lauren whispered.

Claudia turned her back on them. "Claudia Firth on board *Janitor*."

Lauren clutched her head and cried, "Oh, no!"

27

The voice emerged from the loudspeaker again. "Who else is on board?"

"We've got your soldier friend – or whoever he is," said Claudia.

"I need to know who else is with you."

Claudia thought it would be fun to tell this sailor that the others had got away on an inflatable.

He'd have a fit. He wouldn't know what to do. But it wouldn't help. "We're the Anthrax Six," she announced as if she'd just come up with a crazy name for a new band. "What are you going to do about it?"

"Protect the public with all means at our disposal."

While she talked to him, Claudia turned to the others and raised her eyebrows. "But if you go down that road, you're going to look pretty silly."

There were four seconds of radio silence before she got a reply. "Explain."

"Before I set out, I called Sheila Welsh," Claudia said. She paused to allow the officer to ask a question.

"Who is Sheila Welsh?"

"A journalist with a confusing name."

"What do you mean?"

"She should be called Sheila Scott because she's Scottish."

"What's your point?"

"She wrote a story about Betty MacLeod in a book. Betty MacLeod was married to Jack MacLeod. He worked on the island years ago – and you killed him."

"How is this relevant to the present situation?"

"For the last half an hour, I've been sending her messages. Like where we are and what's going on."

This time, the silence was much longer. Eventually, the man replied, "There's been a blackout on phone calls and text messages."

"We know that," Claudia replied. "But you forgot the internet. My mobile – well, my sister's – is connected, and Sheila Welsh has got a *Contact Me* box. They're great. I once wrote to this TV star through her *Contact Me* page. Asked her a question. After a bit, I got an e-mail back. She said her favourite jam was blueberry. Mine's apricot."

"You were telling me about Sheila Welsh."

"Yes. I used the *Contact Me* box on her newspaper's website. I've told her we'll give her our story and

Jack's notebook. I've already sent her some quotes. I bet she's working on a piece right now. So, the secret's out. Getting rid of us won't cover things up any more."

"Stand by, *Janitor*."

She clicked the microphone off, looked at the others and said, "Got them! No problem."

Daniel was astounded. "Are you bluffing or is it true?"

"What do you think?"

"It's brilliant either way," said Mike.

"Did you really call a reporter?" Lauren asked.

"Yep," Claudia said, sitting down again.

"And you've got through to her via the internet?"

Claudia shrugged. "I sent messages, but I don't know if she's got them. It's a *Contact Me* page. You send stuff. It doesn't tell you if anyone's paying attention at the other end."

Lauren nodded slowly. "Fantastic. It's given us

something to bargain with. The only thing we've got to bargain with."

"They're up to something." Mike nodded towards the navy ships. They were on the move again. Two of them were powering straight towards the idling *Janitor*. "They're going to attack!"

"They can't!" Lauren cried. "Not now."

Two of the ships were maintaining their position but the other two were moving in fast. They would be on top of the puny patrol boat in minutes.

"What do we do?" Mike spluttered.

"What *can* we d-do?"

Overhead, thick clouds began to race. The wind was increasing. Claudia gripped the hood as the boat bobbed about on the rising swell. She remembered playing a game called Battleships. It was all about positioning destroyers, submarines and aircraft carriers on a grid like a chessboard. A daft and dull game really. The real thing was far more exciting – and well beyond a game.

The navy boats began to draw apart. One was heading for their starboard side and the other for the port side. At least they weren't going to ram *Janitor*. Not yet.

Claudia and the others watched the monsters lumbering about fifty metres away on either side. Up on deck, sailors checked them out with binoculars.

The tension was unbearable. Claudia was gripping the canopy so tightly that her knuckles were totally white. When both of the towering ships had slid past, the patrol boat rocked even more in their wakes.

The warships were about two hundred metres behind before they slowed and began to wheel round.

"What's happening?" Lauren said.

"Looks like they're surrounding us," Daniel replied. "Making sure we can't make a dash for it."

It was like being at the quiet centre of a storm, waiting for the hurricane to hit.

* * *

It began with a slight vibration and developed into a recognizable sound: the blades of a helicopter slapping the air.

"Oh, no!" Lauren cried. "Not again."

Mike glanced at Daniel. "What's your tactic this time?"

Shaking his head, Daniel watched the approaching aircraft.

The two warships had executed a complete turn. Now, all four ships had their noses pointing directly towards the helpless patrol boat. But it seemed that an RAF helicopter was going to deliver the death blow.

Lauren was looking down, clutching the sides of her head with both hands as if she didn't want to see or hear the missile launch. Mike had stopped gawping at the helicopter. He was kneeling by Annie with her hand in his. Daniel was still at the wheel. Even at this stage, he was probably trying to come up with a way out. Hugh was so white and still that he could already be dead. At the stern, *Janitor*'s skipper had stopped trying to wrench himself free of the rope. Instead he watched the incoming chopper with a look of dread on his face.

28

Daniel was transfixed by the helicopter. This time, he was sure the pilot would have different orders. This time, there would be no opportunity to escape. This time, it would aim to kill. He could even see the missile attached to the side of the aircraft. The chopper came close, withdrew a little and then held its position. All of Claudia's daring counted for nothing.

The noise of the rotors was so loud. Much louder than before. And the sound seemed confused, somehow coming at them from all sides now. Keeping his eye on the sky, Daniel spun round. He gasped when he saw a second helicopter.

"They're making sure," Mike shouted over the din.

Buffeted by the downdraught, Daniel yelled back, "Wait. That one's not... It's not the RAF. It's... something else. A private chopper."

Lauren took her head out of her hands. "What's going on?"

The radio came to life again. This time it was a female voice, almost drowned by the rotor noise. "Sheila Welsh calling Claudia Firth. Is that you? Answer, please, if it's you. Claudia?"

Claudia grabbed the microphone. "Yes, it's me."

"Are you all right?"

"Yes," she replied, yelling into the microphone, "but they're going to kill us."

"Not now I'm here recording it, they're not. They wouldn't dare. I'll speak to them."

To Daniel, the reporter's words, coming unevenly from the radio, could have been the sound of a guardian angel. Sheila Welsh had thrown them a lifeline.

Both helicopters backed off for a few minutes before Sheila spoke to them again. "They're claiming they were just escorting you somewhere safe."

Laughing, Claudia turned the microphone on again. "Funny way of giving safe passage, if you ask me."

"Bearing in mind they'll be listening in on this conversation, can you prove they were doing anything else?"

"Prove it? How?"

Daniel nudged his sister. "I can." At last he had the help and opportunity to use his plan. He took the microphone, introduced himself to the angel hovering noisily overhead and then said, "Before I tell you, what's to stop them sinking us and shooting you d-down?"

Sheila answered, "I'm online to the office and everyone there knows what I'm doing."

"In that case, I've got pictures on my mobile," Daniel said. "I've got video of that RAF helicopter d-destroying our yacht. And I've got stills of animal skeletons and chains, the anthrax bomb site, empty explosive rods, and stuff like that. Plenty to prove everything Claudia's told you. It's all yours if you can get us into an isolation hospital."

"I've been thinking about that," the journalist replied. "Let me negotiate with your...erm...escort. I'll get back to you. Over and out."

Daniel put the microphone down and turned to Claudia. A wave tilted the launch and he staggered forward into her arms. He didn't let go straight away. Instead, he said, "You're a genius, Claudia. A weird one, but d-definitely a genius."

29

When Mike walked into the nursing home two months later, he entered a totally different world. Its inhabitants were quiet and grey and slow and they looked at him as if he were an alien. Maybe some of them recognized him from the newspapers. Since his escape from the island, he'd become well known as one of the Anthrax Three. He didn't have a hope of identifying the woman he'd come to see, but the nurse guided him to the right room.

She flung open a door and said, "Here you are, Betty. The visitor I told you about. Mike."

Betty MacLeod was sitting in an armchair, dressed in thick woollen clothes, with a blanket wrapped around her legs. Mike wondered why she hadn't dissolved in sweat.

"Er…hello." The door closed and Mike walked to the only other chair. He felt awkward. Not knowing how to start the conversation, he took the old photograph out of his pocket and held it out for her.

At first, she didn't look at the picture. She stared into his face as if trying to decide whether he was trustworthy. While she held his gaze, her unsteady wrinkled hand came out and clasped the photo. It was only when she'd got it back on her lap that she looked down at it. At once, an unearthly gasp escaped from her mouth and her hand began to tremble. Eyeing him again, she said, "But this…" She shook her head, unable to continue. Her skin was as dry as crinkled paper but tears rolled down the creases in her face.

"It was in Jack's locker on the island," Mike explained. "It's okay," he added. "It's been disinfected. They can clean things like pieces of paper. It's people who are hard to treat."

"The island. Yes," Betty said. "The nurse told me. And it was in the newspapers."

Mike nodded.

"You were one of the trapped youngsters."

"Yes. We found out what really happened to Jack."

"The papers got hold of his notebook. I read the parts they printed..."

Sheila Welsh had given Jack's decontaminated notebook back to Mike so that he could deliver it to the only person who deserved to keep it. He pulled it from his other pocket and handed it over.

"Yes," Betty mumbled as she opened it up and

glanced at a few of the pages. "It's Jack's writing. Even after all these years..." Overcome, she gripped the notebook and photo in her hands but could not bring herself to look at them any more. "Thank you, young man. I don't know what else to say. Except that... It was the navy that killed him, not the sea. Best to know the truth."

"That's right. They tried to kill us as well. Four times. Even at the end, they pretended they'd come to escort us to land. It was rubbish. They'd have killed us if it hadn't been for Claudia and the reporter."

Betty didn't seem to understand. She said, "I hope you and your friends are all right now. I'd hate to think of you ending up like Jack."

Mike shook his head. "Sheila Welsh got us onto a private island and brought a specialist in. He had to get into a sort of spacesuit to come near us. He gave us injections and stuff. With me, the medicine kicked in before the germ really took hold. I'm lucky, I guess. But..."

Betty leaned forward. "What? What happened?"

Mike sniffed. "We're the same, you and me."

Betty let out a little laugh. It sounded like gargling. "How's that, young man?"

"You lost Jack. I lost…" Mike was determined not to embarrass himself. He tried to stay in control. "Annie didn't make it. I lost my girlfriend."

Betty nodded, acknowledging his grief. "It'll lessen. The pain, I mean." She lifted one fist to her chest. "But keep the memory here."

"Her parents blamed me, I think."

"You?"

"For going to the island."

"Shall I tell you what I think?" Betty said. "People blame the likes of you when the ones who are really to blame are out of reach – or when they don't want to blame themselves."

"It wasn't just Annie. Her brother Hugh was too far gone as well."

"Yes. I remember now. I read about it but…you

know, at my age, it's hard to take it all in. Didn't they say three…?"

"The man who tried to shoot us was fine," Mike replied.

"So, who…?"

Mike took another deep breath. "Annie's sister – the one who saved us – was okay as well. Her little brother, Daniel…"

Betty put out a hand to touch his knee but she couldn't quite reach.

"Daniel was really ill. They said he'd die, but he didn't. He still isn't very well but he's going to be all right. The other one was Lauren. Hugh's girlfriend. She went downhill really fast. The injections made no difference. She didn't stand a chance. They had to cremate the bodies. The Anthrax Six became the Anthrax Three."

Betty's tears came again. This time she seemed to be crying for three young people she didn't even know. She gazed at her guest once more. "Don't you worry. My Jack will look after them. He was a good man."

Mike stood up and wiped his cheeks. "I'd better go now."

"I remember something else from the papers," Betty said. "It's your case that's bringing the Government down. They'll lose the election because of you."

"Looks like it," Mike replied. Then he paused before adding, "It doesn't really matter. No government can give me what I want. No one can bring Annie back."

Daniel leaned on Claudia's shoulders as she sat at her computer and read the headlines that she'd cut and pasted into her latest document. A while ago, he would have asked her why she was keeping those particular news stories. His tone would have suggested that she was wasting her time. Now, he accepted that she found certain topics fascinating and collected them obsessively. He didn't ask why. He would even help.

POISONED ISLAND KILLS THREE TEENAGERS

MAN MURDERS WIFE WITH IRON FOR BURNING HOLE IN HIS BEST SHIRT

TERRORIST BOMBS CLAIM 52 LIVES IN LONDON

TEENAGER GUNNED DOWN FOR WALKING ACROSS NEIGHBOUR'S LAWN

She began to scroll down a newsy website, looking for more reports to add to her murderous file. From over her shoulder, Daniel pointed and said, "Look. *Forbidden island ringed by security fence.*"

"Yeah. But it's not what I'm after." She hesitated and twisted round to face Daniel. "You know, Wikipedia says seventy-two million people died in World War Two. That's wrong. It's seventy-two million and three now."

Daniel did not quibble with her logic. "You're right. So, while you're online, get in there and change it. Anyone can edit Wikipedia. Annie, Hugh and Lauren d-deserve a mention. They're the last three casualties of the war. I hope they're the last anyway."

Claudia smiled. "Okay. Let's do it together."

AUTHOR'S NOTE

This novel was inspired – if that's the right word – by the history of a Scottish island called Gruinard. Until August 1943, Gruinard was used by the British Government for experiments with anthrax. Winston Churchill had proposed a strike with biological weapons on Germany but the German army surrendered before he ordered the release of anthrax spores in Europe. Inhalation of the spores would have caused a rapid and invariably fatal respiratory infection in cattle and humans. After the experiments, Gruinard was quarantined but it was assessed regularly to see whether it was fit for habitation. The spores remained virulent for over forty years. Then the Government decided to take active steps to make the abandoned island safe. Thorough chemical treatment in the 1980s led to decontamination of Gruinard in October 1987.

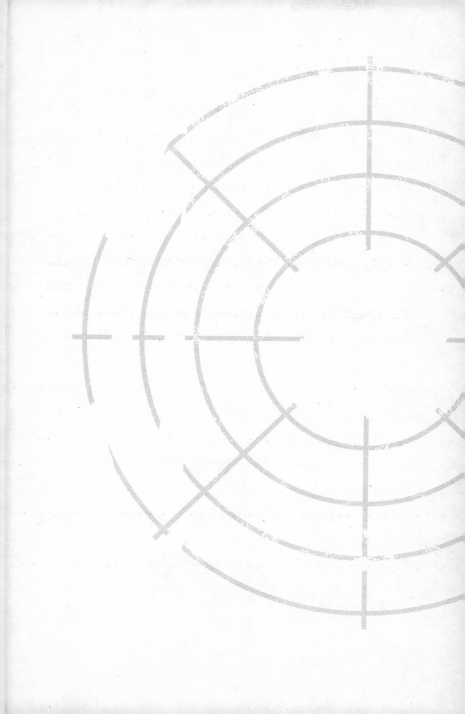

Malcolm Rose was born in Coventry and began his career as a research scientist. He started writing stories while studying for his DPhil degree in chemistry, as a means of escape from everyday life. He is now a full-time writer best known for his gripping science-based thrillers and forensic crime series. He has been awarded the Angus Book Award twice and the Lancashire Children's Book of the Year. His last novel, *Kiss of Death*, was chosen for the national Booked Up reading scheme, and was shortlisted for various prizes, including the Salisbury Schools' Book Award.

For more information about Malcolm Rose visit his website: www.malcolmrose.co.uk

Also by MALCOLM ROSE

KISS OF DEATH

On a school trip to the plague village of Eyam, Seth is moved by the story of how villagers sacrificed their lives to the Black Death. Kim and Wes are more interested in what they see at the bottom of the wishing well – money!

But when they snatch the coins they also pick up something they hadn't bargained for, and as the hideous consequences of their theft catch up with them all, Seth is forced to face a terrifying truth. Has Eyam's plague-ridden past resurfaced to seek revenge?

"Fast-paced, full of nail-biting moments and more than one shock – not for the squeamish."
Primary Times

ISBN 9780746070642

THE TORTURED WOOD

Dillon is struggling to make friends at his new school, and he begins to suspect there's something rotten at the core of the tightknit community, something they're trying to hide.

He finds refuge in the wood that seems to be at the very heart of the mystery. Will the wood give up its dark secret, or is Dillon being drawn into a trap?

Eerie and atmospheric, *The Tortured Wood* is a thriller with a sting in the tale.

"A gripping story... Good spooky stuff."
Adèle Geras, *TES*

ISBN 9780746077436

**FOR MORE SPINE-CHILLING
STORIES, CHECK OUT
WWW.FICTION.USBORNE.COM**